My skin tingled with some kind of feeling I couldn't describe and I stopped in my tracks. I heard someone breathing behind me. If it weren't so quiet, I wouldn't have heard that sound. The hair raised on the back of my neck. I could have sworn no one was close to me.

"Do not turn around. I do not wish to frighten you." The voice was definitely masculine.

I turned around anyway, expecting to see someone, anyone. I saw nothing, nothing but bookshelves with more books.

ALSO BY KARLIE LUCAS

TARRAGON: KEY KEEPER

TARRAGON: DRAGON MAGE

THE UNKNOWN ELF

BOB THE LITTLEST DINOSAUR

Kas

KARLIE LUCAS

DragonKey Press

KAS

DEDICATION

I would like to dedicate this edition of *Kas* to my now departed Grandpa Jackson. There are many things in this book that remind me of. In fact, Kas's grandfather, briefly mentioned in the beginning, is based off of him. The cabin I describe is the cabin I grew up visiting as a child.

The cabin no longer in the family, but this will serve as a reminder of all the wonderful times I had there, sharing them with family, especially my grandpa.

You were an inspiration to me in me in life, and a comfort in death. Your smiles always made my day. And your attention helped an incredibly shy person come out of her shell. You are missed.

KAS

ACKNOWLEDGMENTS

I would like to offer thanks to my family and fans for putting up with me during this whole re-editing process. Thanks to them, I realized I could make this story just a bit better than it was before. For that, I am in your debt.

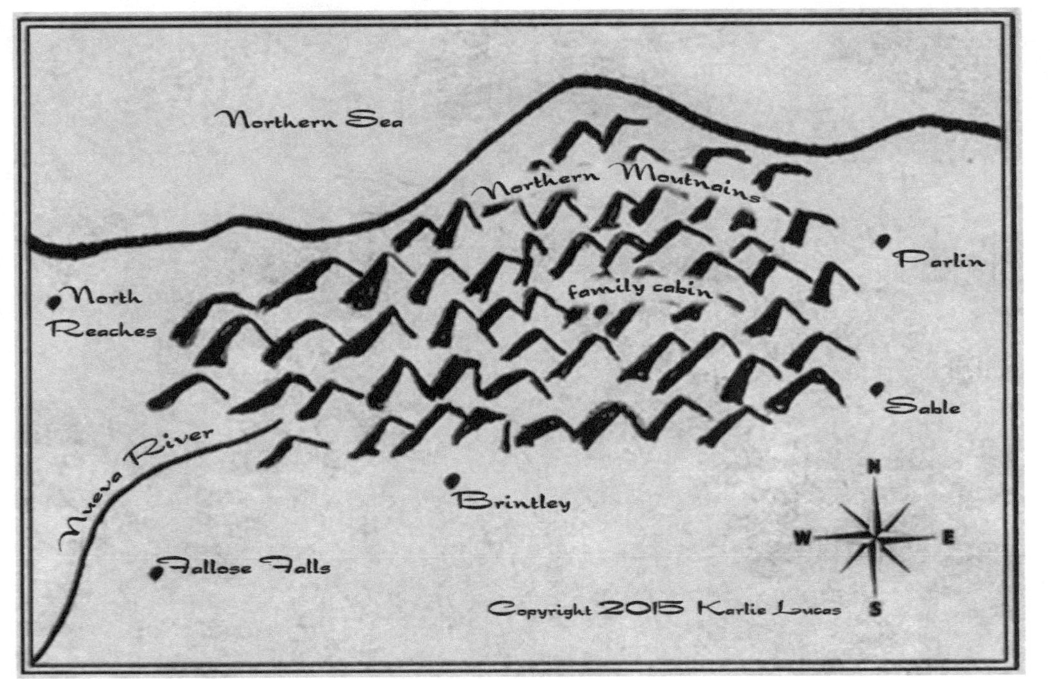

Northern Sea
Northern Moutnains
North Reaches
Parlin
family cabin
Sable
Nueva River
Brintley
Fallose Falls
Copyright 2015 Karlie Lucas
N
W
E
S

KAS

The Waymeet of Worlds

It is a convergence of time and space. It is a meeting of
dimensions, alternate realities, fantasy and reality combined
into one. Anything and everything you have ever dreamed
or hoped for. Everything you have ever feared or despised.
It is here that you learn who you are. It is here that you
find your destiny. Here, all worlds meet. There are but a
few ways to escape its terrible tragedies, or to win over all
possible doubt and failure. The power is inside you, to
conquer your demons or fall by them. This is where you
become who you were born to be.

KAS

KAS

CHAPTER ONE

RED TINGED THE SKY AN unnatural color as I fought my way through a maze of thorns. No matter where I turned, more thorns blocked my path. How was I supposed to get through all of this without killing myself on the briars?

Thunder rumbled through the sky and my breath caught in my throat. Someone else was out there. I had no idea who. But I could hear the crunch of broken branches as whoever it was somehow managed to catch up with me. It was something I knew was a really bad thing. I couldn't let that happen so I ran.

As I ran, dead leaves flew out from behind me. I hoped they'd at least blind the person or thing coming after me, but doubted it. The only thing I could do was run, thorns ripping at my clothes and skin. Why couldn't I just break free?

And then I did break free, stopping short as a cliff cut off abruptly in front of me. What the..? I hastily backed up. This couldn't be happening! Was I going to die? Then a strange beeping noise filled my mind, reminding me of something, though I couldn't immediately place what.

Subconsciously, I rolled over; aiming hit the snooze button on my alarm clock. The insistent sound jarred my brain awake. But instead of finding the button, I felt myself falling, falling in slow motion.

Part of me wanted to scream, but a far stronger part of my mind wouldn't let me. I was too stubborn for that, but it didn't take long before I felt myself hit the ground. It was a shorter span of time than my half-conscious mind thought possible. And with the thump of wood against my backside, my eyes opened.

The light was muted, trapped from completely entering the room I was in. I groaned, wondering if I'd somehow managed to fall out of bed. Again. It was something that seemed to happen more frequently, preceded by the dream of falling. But I was not in my bed and I definitely was not at my college apartment. This was home. I had been sleeping on the couch in the family room. And the oven timer was going off in the kitchen, a room separated from me by a half height wall.

I crawled back onto the sofa and peered over the wall into the next room. Mom was busy stirring up muffin mix she'd made from scratch. Blueberry muffins. Mom was always like that. She insisted that stuff from a box would eventually kill you. I didn't mind the boxed stuff. I hadn't died yet and doubted I would for a good long time. Foods and Nutrition class had settled that debate for me.

I pulled the wrinkled sheet around me and trudged through the kitchen on my way to the family bathroom, which was near the back of the house. Mom didn't seem to notice, even though my sheet swept the little particles of last night's dinner along with me. Dead spaghetti noodles and peas. Mom just ignored the mess. The younger kids never cleaned up after themselves anyway. That was usually left to us older kids, namely me.

There were six of us kids all told. I was the second girl, the third child in the family. There were two boys and one girl under me. The youngest was Russell. He was a two-year-old nightmare waiting to happen. If there was anything he could get into, he did. Without any hesitations. His favorite past time was taking apart Dad's gadgets and Mom's computer. Yet another reason not to live at home during the college years. My computer was safe from him.

I flounced into the bathroom and bolted the door behind me. My older brother, David, would not be waltzing in on me this morning. He had a habit of forgetting he wasn't the only person in the place. His apartment was a single, occupant him.

My older sister, Sara, was the opposite of David. Mostly. She was the favored child, the privileged child. She was always the one who got the car when she had an important date with Mr. So and So in secondary school. No questions asked. Mom and Dad would just hand her the keys, tell her to have a good time, not worrying about it. She got home when she wanted. They didn't do that with me. I figure it just goes to show things aren't always fair. Story of my life.

I hadn't had a single accident during my entire driving career. My sister, on the other hand, had rammed the car into the back of the garage, rear-ended an older couple's car, and crashed into a streetlight. She'd also been pulled over for speeding and running a red light. More times than I can count. I was just glad I wasn't in her shoes, not that things hadn't improved for her. They had. Why couldn't I have been in her shoes?

I looked in the large mirror hanging over the sink and yawned, displaying my far from perfect teeth. Mom kept threatening to tie me up and take me to the dentist if I didn't go soon. On my own. She said I probably needed braces. As if. I didn't like medical doctors. What made her think I'd like dentists? As far as I was concerned, they were all out there just to make money off of other people's suffering. That's why I developed a high tolerance for pain.

I splashed cold water on my face and hoped that would wake my pale skin up. I take after Mom in that right. We are both pale faced in the morning. Not a pretty sight. I pity the man I marry. He'll have a fun surprise on our first morning together. The thought amuses me. My only hope is that I won't get a guy who likes to do nothing but sit in front of the television and down bottles of who knows what. No, that wasn't the type for me.

I wanted an old-fashioned kind of guy, the kind who opened car doors for you, brought you flowers and chocolate kisses once a week. To be honest, I just wanted a guy who appreciated me for me. My sister had dated too many guys who wanted a "Mommy" or a personal slave. I didn't want a guy like that at all, but, for some odd reason, I seemed to attract the same kind of guys. I wished they'd all jump in a lake but where would we put it? Hmmm, the Lake Hope sounds like the perfect place. I've never been to the Lake Hope.

I leaned over the countertop, toothbrush in hand, and stared at my reflection. Mom would say I should put on makeup. Why must we bother with such silly stuff at all? Makeup, in my opinion, is just a waste of time and energy. I looked fine without it. But then I guess I can't hide the fact that I have looks to show off for too much longer.

My eyelids started to droop. I wasn't ready to face the world yet but I tried to keep my eyes open anyway. It was only eight in the morning for crying out loud! Mom would complain that I looked like a raccoon.

Something nagged at the back of my thoughts. If I didn't know any better I'd almost say it was some echo from my dreams. There was always someone else there, someone I couldn't see, calling out to me. Sometimes this person was snarling. Sometimes he was calling out as if he wanted to save me. No matter how hard I tried, I could never see him. But these dreams had been stranger than usual as of late. It wouldn't have surprised me if what I felt now was just a lingering thread from them, tormenting me. They all involved some element of fantasy. Or maybe I was just losing it.

Don't go to the mountains today.

I blinked in surprise and shook my head. What? The Voice seemed to fill my ears. It felt so close, so present in my mind; as if I turned around I might be able to see the speaker.

Do not go to the mountains today.

I double-checked behind the shower curtain to make sure I was alone. The tub was empty and the small bathroom window was closed. Where had that Voice come from?

Don't go to the mountains today.

It sounded like a whisper in my ear, familiar somehow. After a moment, I realized that I recognized it. I had heard it several times before, warning me about things. I'd always listened to it before, but why would it tell me not to go to the mountains today? Then it hit me, like the jarring of machinery coming to life after long inactivity. Or maybe it was stopping. Today was Grandma's birthday. We always celebrated it by going to the family cabin. *In the mountains.* Which were just north of my hometown of Brintley.

Oh great. This warning could be trouble. And I'd been looking forward to this too. I mean, how many days do we get to spend with our grandparents anyway? They aren't going to be around for long, and when they're gone, they're gone. I couldn't let a voice make me miss out on seeing my family could I? Or could I?

Someone started to pound on the door. I could tell by the way the handle was being wrenched that it had to be David. He had no respect for perfectly good doorknobs. He could wait. I had more important things to take care of.

I opened my makeup case, a small one at that, and pulled out some eye shadow. Mom would be so happy. I dabbed on the powder, double dosing my eyebrows with the darkest color, just to make sure she noticed. I finally left the bathroom, after I'd let my brother pound on the door for several more minutes. He slugged me in the arm on my way out.

"Hey!" I complained as I trailed back into the family room, rubbing at my bruised person. I'd get him back later. If I remembered, though my mind was too busy to give it too much thought. The Voice nagged at me, asking me to promise it I wouldn't go to the mountains today. I felt a sense of urgency in the request that almost frightened me. I tried to push it back in my mind, and, at the same time tried to put on some clean clothes. It didn't make things easy but I was determined. Might as well look decent at my own funeral, I decided. I didn't know if I would do the killing or if it would be Mom. Didn't matter either way. Someone would die before the day was out, I was sure.

I reentered the kitchen and was almost mowed over by Russell, who was sporting a sagging diaper. I hadn't even heard him get up. The next child in line, Allisa, was trying to catch him. She had a comb in her hand, for decided use on her prey. She looked like she needed the comb far more than he did. Her hair was a rat's nest of yellow. Talk about total bed head.

My other younger brother entered next. His hair wasn't quite as bad as Allisa's. Not that that was saying much. But then his hair was shorter. He still needed a haircut. He flopped down onto a chair and yawned, showing off teeth that had far more damage than a fourteen-year-old deserved. Cavities galore. Mom should get after him about the dentist. Gotta love Dan. I joined him in the next seat over.

Dad had just started a package of bacon to sizzling in a pan when Sara decided to grace us with her presence. She came up the stairs, her robe trailing out behind her like she was some regal queen, above all her subjects in all things. She would be the lucky one to get the only finished room in the basement, a cubicle to be honest, but still some privacy. But then she was also married. Her husband would probably make his appearance soon. Leave it to Sara to be the first to get married. I had to smile. Grimly. I was surprised no one seemed to notice. But then that's my family for you.

It wasn't a bad match by any means. The two complemented each other. Ron was a psychiatrist. She was in marketing. She advertised his office and he kept her sane, supposedly. I'm not sure how it all worked out but at least they got along. Personally, I didn't see the thrill of psychology. I flunked every class I took.

Ron definitely didn't get points for his looks, either. I couldn't call him handsome; no matter how hard I tried. For Sara's sake. Oh, he didn't look ugly, but he wasn't a drop dead gorgeous guy either. He had sandy colored hair, hazel eyes, and stood about six feet tall, and as skinny as a rail. He looked good when he stood by Sara. She looked a lot like him.

I think I'm the only member of our family who doesn't have light colored hair; something I think went back to my great-grandmother. Every picture I could find of her suggested black hair. But then they were black and white photos, which wasn't all that helpful. My hair was dark brown with red highlights. Mom called it auburn.

"Time to eat," Mom announced as she set a plate piled high with muffins on the table. We never starved at home. Ever.

Mom took her customary seat near the head of the table, Dad sitting opposite her. They exchanged a wink and a knowing smile. They were probably playing footsy under the table. I wished I had someone to play footsy with. The idea of Ron and Sara doing that, however, turned that thought off in a flash. In fact, I wanted to gag.

My other siblings played musical chairs until most of them were satisfied. Since I was unwilling to move, I got squeezed in-between Dan and Sara's husband, Ron. They both smelled of boy. Dad said grace and everyone started to dig in like there was no tomorrow, passing butter and bacon. I just waited for the feeding frenzy to subside before attempting to snag some food for myself.

The usual breakfast chatter ensued, which I tried to ignore. Our cat, Sammy, wove around my legs, begging for some food. I dropped him a few bits of bacon and he purred in appreciation. Man, I missed that cat. I'd come home if only to see the cat. My siblings claimed him as theirs but he technically belonged to me. My apartment didn't allow pets.

"There are a few things we need to cover," Dad began. It might as well have been the droning of a fly for all the attention he was getting. "I don't want Russell to be allowed to just run at will while we're up there," Dad stated. Or was he reprimanding? I couldn't tell. He was always more serious and quiet than Mom. "It took almost an hour to find him last time because someone wasn't watching him." I turned my head just in case he was looking at me. "Someone has to keep an eye on him if he goes outside the cabin. That's your job, Kas."

Arg! Why was it always me? Why couldn't Dan or even Sara do it? She could use the practice for when she had her own kids, whenever that would be. I just got too caught up in my daydreams and fantasy worlds to keep my attention focused on the pest. He had more energy than I did and it sure kept me in constant exercise to watch him. It made me tired, something that wasn't good for my writing. After all, a tired mind can't write, right? I slumped in my chair, arms folded.

Kas, keep your promise.

Oh joy, the Voice again. I hadn't actually promised it anything, except that I'd try. If Mom said I was going then I was going, Voice or no Voice. I wanted to see the leaves before they fell anyway. Why did it have to make things so hard? I pushed the scrambled eggs around my plate, gathering courage.

"Mom?" I took a deep breath and she looked up, her expression a quizzical one. Her eyes locked onto mine and I found myself feeling lightheaded. Maybe it was because I somehow forgot how to breathe. "I don't want to go." I let out all the air in my lungs.

It was like someone had hit a pause button. Total silence. She nodded once or twice as I sunk down into my chair. Now I'd done it. She glanced towards Dad, her forehead creasing. "Why? Don't you want to see Grandma and Grandpa?"

Guilt trip! Why! I felt like screaming in a melodramatic manner but withstood the temptation. It wouldn't have gotten me anywhere. That only worked for Sara. "I do want to see them, but I can't go today. I have plans." I hated it when she used that tone.

"Sweetie, Grandma expects us all to be there. You wouldn't deny her what could possibly be the last time she'll see you, do you? She could die any day, you know. Besides, you asked for the day off. You told me yesterday on the phone."

Oh great, she'd remembered. And she had to pull the "grandma might die any day now" card out of her deck. It wasn't fair! I was half-glad but also half-backed into a corner. "I know I don't work but I don't feel I should go. There's just something not right about it."

"You're not sick are you?"

"No."

"Then what's wrong?"

I sunk even lower in my chair. There was no way she would make me bring this out into the open was there? Not now! I groaned to myself but the expression on her face didn't allow ignoring her. My voice was just a whisper, my throat dry as I spoke; hoping Ron would suddenly go deaf. "My little Voice warned me." I glanced at Ron. His eyebrows pricked up. Great. He knew.

"Well, I don't see any reason for that to keep you from celebrating with your family." Mom picked up her abandoned muffin and spread real butter on it; an act that meant the conversation was over.

I bowed my head, resting my forehead on the edge of the table. Man! This was not going where I wanted it to, but then I wasn't sure where I wanted it to go anyway. I might as well throw caution to the wind now. "But it was the Voice, Mom. It's always been right before." What I was trying to say was "tell me I have to go, please." That way I would have kept my promise to the Voice, at least about trying, and it would be final. I really did want to go. I didn't dare glance at Ron.

Mom looked at me with pity in her brown eyes. "Honey, no voice is going to get in the way of spending time with our family. I want you to come anyway." And this time her tone brooked no arguments. Dominant mothers. Gotta love 'em. Most of the time.

I wanted to cheer. I wanted to dance, stick out my tongue, act insanely nasty, like a two-year-old. Like Russell. But what if there was a good reason not to go? If that was true then I'd made a mistake and could only cross my fingers, hoping nothing would happen. Either way, things were not good. My days were numbered now. I could tell. Ron was leaning towards Sara, whispering with excitement.

Kas.

"I know, I know," I muttered to the Voice. My stomach flip-flopped with acid and I excused myself from the table, a headache forming behind my eyes. I stalked into the family room and flopped down on the couch. There was nothing I could do about this whole situation. I was doomed no matter which direction I turned. And I'd thought being in secondary school was hard! So glad I wasn't anymore.

I had given my word to go now, more or less. I couldn't back down. And now Ron knew that it was possible I was an unstable person because of all this. I could hear him whispering to Sara with less restraint. Oh what fun he'd have trying to analyze me. I'd be his lab rat forever after this. I wished I could just drop through the floor as if I'd never existed.

David invaded my privacy some time later, though I wasn't sure exactly how long it had been. Probably long enough for him to finish his own food. He once told me the most depressing sight in the world was an empty plate. My own stomach held a few pieces of bacon and some fragments of egg but nothing else. He sat down on the couch, almost on my feet. "Hey." I could feel the couch tip towards his end as he sat down.

"Hey." I didn't feel like talking.

"You okay?"

I shook my head, not to say no, but just because I didn't know what to say. I breathed out with an exaggerated sigh and pursed my lips. "Why does Mom have to be... such a Mom? I hoped she'd not make me bring up the whole Voice thing, just take my words for face value and pronounce I had to go. That's all she had to say." I didn't add that I'd managed to keep the whole thing a secret from Ron all this time, only a year, but still. Why had Mom made me break that most strenuous of oaths I'd taken to never tell him?

David laughed, all ease and humor. How could he do that so easily? It wasn't even remotely fair. "Maybe because she *is* a Mom?"

I had to laugh a bit with him. Only a bit. I wasn't sure why I was laughing, but it seemed appropriate. I wasn't paying strict attention, but at least he was trying to cheer me up. Maybe I wouldn't get him back for hitting me after all. Maybe. I couldn't laugh for long. I's never been able to. There usually wasn't anything to laugh about.

"Now Ron will try all kinds of psycho stuff on me." I snuggled up into the cushions, feeling sorry for myself. It was funny how my brother could change in what felt like a blink of an eye. It always amazed me. I only wished I could drop my anger like he seemed to be able to do. It sure would help. My temper had always gotten me into trouble.

"Sorry about keeping you out of the bathroom," I said after a while. "I just woke up on the wrong side of the couch I guess."

David cuffed me on the ear. "Don't worry about it. I could have used Mom and Dad's, but why give them more worries? I think having a twenty-eight-year-old son who isn't married yet, or even dating for that matter, is enough, don't you? Besides, what would Ron say?" He winked.

CHAPTER TWO

THE JOURNEY UP INTO THE mountains was rather uneventful, unfortunately. I'd hoped for a road slide or something, anything to send my torment, but no dice. I sat in the back seat of the family van with Dan and David, burying my nose in a book. I didn't get too far in though. My stomach had started to churn and I swear it got worse the farther up we went. I wanted to be sick. And I know it wasn't from motion sickness.

The dirt road leading to the cabin was muddy. It was a good thing the van had four-wheel-drive. It had rained only yesterday and I didn't like the way the clouds seemed to skulk around the higher peaks.

I felt my stomach drop into my shoes. I knew its contents would burst out and ooze all over the place as soon as I set foot out of the car. Not that anyone would notice, even if that did happen.

We arrived, the last family to make it to the cabin. As a result, we ended up blocking everyone else's cars into the driveway, including Ron and Sara's. They'd come up a bit ahead of us in their own vehicle. Our stopping splashed mud up on the white frame. I almost felt cheerful about that. They couldn't leave until we did.

I was the last one out of the car, trudging in inch deep muck. I picked my way to the cabin steps and tried to not slip on the more sodden areas. I could see a section or two where someone had fallen victim to the treacherous slime. Their skid marks lay like a silent warning to the unwary.

I navigated the wet steps without mishap and entered the drafty cabin. Grandpa had started a fire in the old heater and my aunts were busy peeling vegetables. We'd be having cast-iron cooked potatoes tonight if they had anything to do with it. Slow cooked to perfection. They'd even brought a whole turkey to go with it, marinated in lemon-lime soda the night before. I guess it was supposed to make it taste better or something. Dad went over to the counter and helped the uncles shape meat patties. Hamburgers were on the lunch menu, grilled.

Finished with the heater, Grandpa tried getting his portable grill to light and I volunteered to help, but he declined. I guess he still remembered the incident from last year. I'd accidentally set his favorite chair on fire while trying to start the real fire with a lighter. It wasn't my fault he'd left that stupid thing so close to the fire pit.

David disappeared with the older cousins outside and Sara and Ron joined those at work in the kitchen. Russell had found a toy wheelbarrow and was content to just push it around the front room. He mowed down anyone who happened to cross his path. Allisa headed straight for the dolls and I situated myself on an old recliner with an even older comic book.

After a while, one of my uncles came over and tried to make small talk. I guess they kicked him out of the kitchen for snitching in the cheese. I tried to pay attention but couldn't. My stomach was twisting into knots of anticipation. Not that happy anticipation but that anxious anticipation when you know your doom is at hand. Someone once told me if I didn't stop thinking things like that I'd die at a young age. As if seventeen was all that young. I don't know if it was true, but it might not matter after today anyway.

My uncle started to talk about the weather and how it might affect his plumbing business. Plumbing, great. Now there was a real topic of interest. But I felt my mind roaming again. I tried to direct my attention back at him as he related his last exploit with the plunger. It was something about how he'd turned the water off to a whole apartment to fix the pipes. The only thing that made it interesting was that there was some guy who came out in a towel asking when he'd have the water back on. I guess the guy had been in the shower at the time.

My continued attempts to pay even the smallest bit of attention were unsuccessful. After several more failed minutes of inattention on my part, I excused myself and headed outside. He didn't seem to notice. Let Dan watch the younger ones. He was only playing pick-up sticks with those near his age. He could handle it.

Mom saw me as I tried to make my escape. "Where are you going?" she asked.

"For a walk. The fresh air might help get rid of my headache," I explained, hoping she would accept that excuse.

"There's some medicine in the emergency kit if you need it," she responded. And then she went right back to shaping meat patties as if nothing had interrupted her activities. It was weird, unlike her somehow. But I only nodded and went outside.

Soon, I was walking down one of my favorite paths, trying not to think about it. My day was weird enough. The path was lined with late wild flowers in pinks, whites, and yellows. I hoped looking at them would help me forget about that warning and Mom's weird behavior.

You should not have come.

"Oh go buzz off. Jump in a lake." I stormed down the trail, lengthening my pace, hoping my pounding heart would drown it out. Too bad I wasn't any good at sports or I'd have run. I needed to let my emotions out but didn't feel I could with the Voice listening in. I couldn't run away from it anyway, even if I'd wanted to. After all, how do you runaway from something inside your head?

After having walked some ways, I came across the Sitting Rock. It was my private little place to sit and think. The rock was more of a stone; the majority of it being brown and gray in color. It sat half-submerged in the soil but was still pretty good sized on top. You could set up a little two-person picnic on it with room to spare. The best part was that it had large grooves that made great places to sit.

I sat down and let the tears come, or, rather, I tried to let them come. I hadn't cried in years. A book I once read had a character that refused to cry because it was a waste of resources. I'd been stupid at the time and agreed with her. I wished now that I hadn't. I'd trained myself to not cry so well that I couldn't anymore and I wanted to cry. No. I *needed* to cry.

I squeezed my fists into my eyes, shutting out the world, turning my vision red and dark blue. This was all so confusing and frustrating. Why didn't someone want me up here today? Had I tipped the hands of fate and chosen my path into forever? Why wouldn't that stupid Voice tell me something *useful?*

I felt a cold splotch of water touch my arm. I unscrewed my fists from my eyes and looked up. The clouds had moved, were still moving, closing in and growing darker. I stood up and a sudden wave of intense dizziness filled me. It had to be vertigo or some other instability caused by having my eyes pressed so tightly shut. Either way, I turned and grasped at the rock for dear life so I wouldn't fall over. It felt like my body was trying to tear itself apart from the inside out.

Thunder cracked overhead and I closed my eyes again, keeping them shut with all my might, willing my body to stay in one piece. I felt like I was on one of those old merry-go-rounds they used to have at the parks. Of course, that was before they decided they were too dangerous and took them out. I was spinning, spinning out of control. And then everything suddenly lurched.

I told you, silly girl. I told you.

I felt the ground falling out from under me, first the rock, then the soil. I didn't know if anything else was falling. I was too afraid to open my eyes. Everything felt like it was crumbling under me. Everything. I fell for who knows how long, definitely much longer than I had this morning. Much longer than I had in my recent dreams. I began to wonder if I'd fall into forever. And then... Thud!

My head jarred and I had to open my eyes. I was lying on the ground, only two feet from the rock. I could see it out of the corner of my eye. I pushed myself up and looked around. Everything looked just the same. The rock was still imbedded in the soil. The pines were still arching their branches over my little spot. The aspen trees still held their changing leaves out for inspection. The clouds were still drawing closer together. And it was raining.

I rolled my head to see if I'd done any damage to my neck but only felt some slight stiffness. And other than having had the wind knocked from me, I felt fine. I shivered, a cold breeze running against my back. Maybe I'd caught something and was getting sick. I should go back.

Turning the appropriate direction, I started out but felt the dizziness fill me again. It was so bad I had to stop and close my eyes or be sick. When I opened them again, I was facing the other side of the path. I turned around one more time and the same thing happened. I wanted to scream. I felt like I was in some freaky house of mirrors.

I wanted to kick out at something. Instead, I scuffed my shoes against the mud. "All right, you stupid force of nature, or whatever you are! I get the hint!" I started to walk down the trail that led further away, almost jogging. I realized I was getting further from the cabin, brash in my decision to follow some unseen force's idea of what I should be doing. But all the dizziness, queasiness, and other discomforts immediately left me. All but the anxiety. That doubled. I thought my heart would burst with how hard it was pounding.

The scenery looked about the same as it always did, spruce, pine, and a few thorny bushes here and there. There were even some aspen trees that thinned out until they disappeared. But even the familiarity didn't comfort me because something in the back of my mind told me it was wrong, all wrong.

I walked for about ten minutes in this direction, noticing the trees were changing. They were growing taller, thicker, more shaggy. Their bark was harsher to look at, more gray than it should be. And the shadows around the roots were deeper than they should be. It was kind of eerie, to be honest.

Maybe it was only a trick of the rain or the light. Maybe it was just me being paranoid. I realized I should have run into a neighbor's cabin by now but hadn't. And that thought was too weird for me to deal with right now.

The farther I walked the more the trees changed and the harder my heart pounded. This anxiety would be the death of me. Was that what the Voice had tried to warn me about? That I'd somehow let my paranoia kill me up here?

After a while, the rain let up but the sky remained dark, and was growing darker. Tendrils of deep-blue mist hung near the trees' roots. It looked like something out of a horror movie. The trees were also more gnarled now; their leaves and needles had fallen to the ground. They were dead trees. I see dead trees. Great. I was losing it.

I started to look up at the empty branches as I walked, until I stumbled over something and had to look down. The path had faded in front of me. I looked back and found the same result. No path. When had it disappeared? Just barely? Or had it been gone for a while and I just hadn't noticed until now? I was on the verge of losing it. Maybe I already had.

The ground was covered in rough stones and broken twigs. Puddles of water lay near the trees, spreading little fingers out towards me, as if curious, or menacing.

"Kas."

It was not the same voice that now called my name. Not the voice I'd heard in the bathroom, the voice I was mad at right now. This voice held more echoes to it. It jumped around, from trunk to trunk, not inside my ear. Or was it jumping around in my head?

"Kas."

It was a breath of air, slight enough to just leave a feeling of something that almost tingled. It was like the lightest strands of cobweb had brushed against my skin. I tried to shrug it off but it wouldn't leave me alone. It snuggled up next to my brain and stayed there, like a porcupine turned to kitten habits, except it didn't hurt. I could feel it curling up inside my skull, purring but jabbing at the same time, jabbing towards the right side of my head. I turned that way and the jabbing centered to my forehead.

I took a step and the purring increased. The jarring porcupine stopped poking after several more steps in that direction. The purring continued so I kept walking. This was beyond weird now, and the fact that I'd stopped questioning everything didn't help calm my racing heart.

A twig snapped behind me. I whirled around but didn't see anything but my breath came too fast anyway. I put a hand to my chest to try and force my lungs to relax. Once my breathing was more or less under control, I continued on the path this new voice had chosen for me. I didn't know what else to do. My Voice was being strangely silent. Had I offended it? A small part of me worried that I had, but another part was glad it was gone. And that confused me too.

A wolf called out and I hugged my wet shirt closer around me, goose bumps running around my skin. I heard another twig snap, and the faint breath of someone behind me. My mind raced. "Don't turn around. Don't turn around. Just run," it seemed to say but I hesitated. My limbs were frozen. "Run, you idiot. Run!"

The almost yelled advice woke me from my paralysis and I ran. I realized, only after I'd started into some disjointed stride of panic, that I'd been the one to yell. And not just in my mind, but out loud. I didn't even look back to see what I was running from. The panic felt too strong.

The tree branches tried to grab at my clothing but couldn't without grabbing me too. I wouldn't let them grab me. But, after a while, they didn't seem to bother with that. I felt like they had changed their goal and were now trying to trip me. That thought alone made me run all the harder.

I heard my breath now, coming in short gasps. I didn't know how much more my body could take. I imagined myself being chased by a pack of hungry wolves, which gave me added speed, adrenaline pumping through my veins.

The trees seemed to reach farther and my ears fancied the sounds of voices calling out. It was some strange language that sounded unnatural to my ears. And there, in the background, was the sound of wolves howling. A root lifted of its own accord and tripped me, the rocks dancing to stand in my way. I was still falling, even after I'd hit the ground.

CHAPTER THREE

SOMETHING HELD ME DOWN SO that I couldn't move. I couldn't look around because my eyes didn't want to open. Soft cloth met my fingers as I clenched my fists. My head hurt. I wasn't sure if any other parts of me did too or not.

My first thought was that I was sick and then that I'd slept in. I wondered why no one had woken me up. I recalled having been at the cabin, but all the beds there were as hard as rocks. This one was soft, like a feather. I was floating on a dream. To be honest, it felt pretty nice. I wasn't sure I wanted to move though.

Now that I was more or less aware of my surroundings, I realized I heard voices in my head. They were arguing over something. I couldn't tell what it was about, but I didn't like what they were saying. I was sure I was only coming in on the tail end of the conversation. I probably would have been confused by what they were saying anyway. It made no sense to me.

"You may have won for now but you will not win forever. I will have her and you will bow before me like the worm you are!"

"You shall not have her or me, demon."

"We shall see, little one. But I drove her to this. You see? I am not as powerless as you may have thought. I can destroy her from within and you will be powerless to stop me."

"If you harm her--"

"Careful, princeling, wouldn't want to lose your temper would you? What would your subjects say?"

"You will leave her be. I command you."

"Never. She is mine!"

My eyes flew open, as if released from some kind of spell. I admit I expected to see the two arguing men standing in front of me, or maybe to the side of the bed, but my gaze was met only by shadows tinged with firelight. The flames danced in a large fireplace, highlighting ornate objects scattered around the room. Their shadows were warped but there were no men. Or anything that resembled one.

I looked around and found myself on a bed with what had to be a silk canopy. A small table lay just to the left. It contained a plethora of brushes, a few combs, even more ribbons, and a mirror. There was also an old-fashioned ewer in what I guessed was some kind of washbowl. Both had a floral pattern, but not from any flower I recognized.

When I surveyed myself I was in for a shock. I no longer wore a pair of blue jeans and a purple button-up shirt. I was decked in heaps of deep-green fabric sewn into an elegant but gaudy dress. It looked like something you find only in a romance movie or novel. My feet were even encased in silk slippers of the same hue. And I was wearing a necklace with a dangling green jewel. I would have rolled my eyes if I'd known what was going on.

A large oil lamp sat on a table near the fireplace. I hurried to light it, throwing back bedding and trying not to trip over the high heels. I hoped the lamp would supply enough light to see the whole room. I was forgetting that even the lamps Mom had at home didn't fill the bathroom with complete light. But any additional light had to be better than just the firelight, I reasoned.

A small flint lay by the lamp's side. I didn't have a clue how to use it so I took a long stick I found on the mantelpiece and stuck it into the fireplace until the end caught fire. I had to keep one hand on the outer wall so I didn't fall in. But even with that precaution, the drafts from the flames were still hot against my skin.

Trimming the wick, I sent a silent word of thanks to Mom. If she hadn't kept a collection for emergencies, I might have burned up the entire room trying to get the lamp lit. Even with my basic knowledge of wick lighting, it took me a few minutes to get it to burn just right. But when I did, its light fell on an open wardrobe full of dresses. I hurried over, hoping to find something less gaudy than what I already had on, like my own clothes, but that wish was vain.

I succeeded in finding a dress that was more or less plain. I could have worn it to church, except it did have a few jewels sewn to the bodice. It still reached all the way to the floor and had a full skirt; even though it was the only dress I could consider being suitable. Everything else was covered in lace. I shudder to think about all that…! That…! Ugh! I put the dress on and left the green slippers on the floor where I'd thrown the other gown. I couldn't resist staring heavenward and rolling my eyes since I'd refrained earlier. What was this world coming to? Why weren't there any pants?

I carried the lamp towards the tall drapes that seemed to frame every wall, except for one. The curtains were patterned with little cupid figures in various poses. And they all wore a little diaper round the middle, for which I was thankful. Dad raised us to believe in not over-exposing our flesh to anyone, males especially. Most of the guys I knew had dirty minds anyway, including Ron. I pulled back a few inches of drapery, allowing a crack of light to enter the room, but only a small amount.

Snow fluttered past the thick pane of glass. The window seemed warped as if from some intense heat. It distorted the landscape outside so I couldn't see out of very well. I could only tell that the ground was covered in white and that the sky was still overcast. I had no clue what time it was. I left the windows to explore the room further.

A hardwood table lay parallel to the outward wall. A high-backed chair faced the windows, pushed under the edge of this table. On the table was a sheaf of parchment, an ink well and a quill pen. Near the fireplace was a bookshelf about as tall as I was and just about as wide. The shelves were, for the most part, empty. I didn't recognize any of the titles that were there. The leather binding them was also strange, some odd texture I wasn't familiar with. It felt like plastic, but not quite like plastic. It had a fabric-like feel to it. But the spines smelled the same as the hardbound tomes I was used to reading.

My bare feet felt the odd texture of raised paisleys on the tiling near the fireplace. There was a wide area there with no carpeting whatsoever. The tiling didn't match the carpet's cabbage pattern of blues and greens. A rocking chair faced the fire, resting on the edge of the carpet. It was the old-fashioned kind you could sink into and not be able to get back out of easily.

A loud knock sounded from somewhere near the middle of the solid wall where a large, possibly oak, door stood in an ornate frame. The sound, after so much silence, seemed deafening and my heart jumped. I contemplated taking a minute or two to calm my rapid pulse. Instead, I ran over and reached for the silver handle. I hoped I could somehow keep it from turning. I told myself I didn't know how many more surprises I could take. Maybe I could wait them out. I assumed it was a person. My mind refused to accept anything else. But someone had already turned the knob from the other side.

The door opened faster than I could bar it, even though it was only wide enough to allow one person through. My hand fell from the handle as a rather young woman, dressed in some old-fashioned maid costume of green and white, stood in the doorway. I took a step back, not daring to trust my eyes, which were probably bugging out.

"Miss." She curtsied, acting all casual, as if everything here was just so… commonplace. As if this was normal. I stared at her and wrinkled my eyebrows. She didn't look dangerous. Completely the opposite, in fact. I wasn't sure if I liked her or not.

Deciding to dispense with pleasantries, I went right to the meat of the matter. "Who are you?"

She curtsied again. "I am Jenny and the Master has assigned me to be your lady in waiting. If there is anything I can do for you, please do not hesitate to ask." I could tell she meant every word.

I took another step back and she followed me into the room, closing the door behind her. If anything, I'd have her stop curtsying to me. It was downright weird.

"Right." I edged over to the desk and chair, sitting down on the padded furniture. I wondered just how much information she'd give me if I pumped her. I decided starting out with the situation at hand would be best.

"So, could you tell me if this is reality or some psychotic dream I'm having? Because the last thing I remember is walking in a dark wood where it was raining, not snowing. And if this is some psychotic dream, could you please direct me to the nearest exit? Because I really want off this merry-go-round."

My words didn't seem to faze her, even though I felt they should have. "I understand your confusion. The

Master had you brought here," Jenny explained. "One of his hunting parties found you in the woods." Again, her tone was too commonplace, too... I don't know. Normal, I guess.

I nodded and wrinkled up my forehead even more, thinking about this in present terms. Hunting parties? Was she talking about some kind of party full of chips and alcohol to aid in your hunting? Was it some kind of male bonding thing? That's what my dad would have said at any rate. He didn't allow any kind of alcohol in the house, period. But if I were having some kind of delusion about more... medieval times, it would make more sense. They didn't have real hunting parties anymore, did they? Not like in the fantasy and history books I read. Right?

"You were soaked to the bone," Jenny continued. "And you had on the strangest garments I have ever seen. It took me the longest time to remove them."

My eyes bugged out even more and my jaw dropped. "You... undressed me?" I couldn't think of any better way to say it as my voice squeaked on the last word.

Jenny shrugged like it was nothing. "You were soaked. We had to remove those clothes before you caught a chill."

"We?" I tried to gulp down my spit, coughing a bit as it hit that one spot at the back of my throat. I tried to contain it, which only made my face red, but I was not going to cough anymore then I had to in front of her. Catch a chill. Wow.

Jenny shrugged. "Several other maids aided me in the task. The buttons and other modes of fastening completely baffled me." She said this all like it were nothing at all. What kind of place had I landed in? Was this the nut house, something Ron had set up to punish me for speaking to little voices?

"So, this is just a dream right? I mean this can't be real." I shook my head. It ached even to think about the possibility, not that it didn't already.

"Oh no, miss. This is no dream. You are fully awake."

Great. I slumped forward, ruining the guise of perfect posture I'd tried to keep. So much for that theory. I ran a hand through my hair, snagging my fingers on the golden pins someone had put in. I pulled one out and played with it.

"No, it can't be real. This is a dream. I hit my head on a rock and this is the end result. There can't be any other rational explanation." Unless the loony bin idea was true, but even that was a bit farfetched. Of course, I could also be dead and this was my punishment for secluding myself so much from everyone else.

Jenny smoothed her apron, bending down to my eye level. "It is true that you injured your head, but I assure you that you are fully conscious. Everything you see around you is real." Was she playing the maternal card, like Mom always did when she wanted me to believe something?

I heard the music from one of those mystery shows running through my head. I felt like looking around the room suspiciously but didn't. This was ridiculous. This couldn't be right. There was no way this was happening. It was a fairy tale. A dream. A fantasy. Had I finally lost all sense of sanity? Ron would say I had. But what could I do except play along? Maybe *I* wasn't the delusional one.

"Where am I?"

Jenny returned to her full standing position, all five feet of it. I was taller than her by several inches. "You are in the castle of Mantaset, Waymeet of Worlds. The Master rules over this realm as well as several adjoining this convergence."

I blinked in confusion. What was she talking about? What was this Waymeet of Worlds? I'd never heard of such a place in my life, real or imagined. And what in tar was a convergence? This was nonsense. I felt dumb. Maybe I should have taken physics like my dad had suggested.

"I know this may seem confusing to you," Jenny continued. It felt like she had some kind of extra sensory perception. Or a script. Either that or it was written across my face, as clear as day. "The Master knew it would be thus, but your being here cannot have been an accident. No one comes here unless they are bidden or sent for. Not even I understand everything because I was brought here as well."

I shivered, pulling my arms around my chest for warmth. The crackling fire didn't seem to add any comfort, even though fires had always calmed me. It was the way the flames danced, intertwining with each other in some intricate form. It was like a waltz. I could have easily become a pyro. Maybe it would have been better that way. Just let the castle burn, and this psycho dream with it. Was it really a castle?

"I know you have questions. That is why the Master has requested I show you to the library where he will meet you."

I admitted, to myself only, that questions floated around, disjointed, but still there. I couldn't make sense of them all. Practical things like "what was the layout of this place?" and "who was the Master?" ran through my head, and many others far less practical, like "what is Jenny talking about?" I felt I needed some kind of grasp on this situation I obviously didn't have. Things were slipping through my fingers. And where he will meet *me*? Wasn't I going to meet *him*?

Jenny opened the door, beckoning for me to follow. I got up from the chair and stuck the pin back in my hair, probably out of place. I didn't feel like I had a choice anyway, so I let her lead me into the hallway. They probably had contingency plans for things like that.

The corridor was at least six feet wide and two stories tall, like the room we had just come from. The tall part I mean. The carpeted floor was soft. My feet didn't feel any discomfort. I was glad what I was wearing covered my feet. That way Jenny couldn't see they were bare. It might be taboo. After all, they'd had me wearing shoes in bed. I hoped that wasn't something they expected to continue.

I didn't realize I was just standing there, staring, until she inclined her head to indicate that I should follow her. At least she didn't try to grab my hand. That would have been awkward.

Jenny led me down several different hallways. I saw the occasional person polishing armor or dusting picture frames. Several doors opened up on either side of us but I didn't feel I should pry into them by looking. She slowed her pace, giving me time to look around. I guess she didn't miss the look that had crossed my face. Either that or this Master wasn't in a hurry to meet me. I couldn't be sure which was the case.

I walked up to a portrait that looked more like a modern photograph than paint on canvas. It was a picture of a young man in some simple but flowing clothes. He wore a Robin Hood kind of outfit, right down to the dashing, yet not overbearing green color. He had a charming smile and sparkling green eyes that laughed with mirth. I wanted to know this man for the mere sake of knowing him. There was something compelling about his eyes. I feared that if they were real, I'd drown in them.

I shook myself free from the portrait and caught up with Jenny. She had turned around to see where I'd gotten. I smiled sheepishly and followed without letting my eyes wander any further than the carpet. The weave of it was so odd that it was like following a maze with my eyes. I got so caught up in it that I bumped into Jenny when she stopped in front of a wide set of double doors.

"Here is where I leave you. When the Master has finished speaking with you, I will be waiting just outside these doors to lead you back to your room." She curtsied again and stood to one side. I thought she said everything deliberately, as if I needed her to be absolutely clear about her intentions. Maybe I did.

"You're not coming in?" I could feel my heart starting to thump in my chest. Even though I didn't know who she was, or what her real intentions were, I didn't like the thought of parting from her. The idea of being alone with some strange male filled me with an emotion I didn't want to feel. I'd felt enough of it in the last day or two and I didn't want any more of it.

"I am not allowed inside," she explained.

I looked at her with apprehension. Who knew what waited for me past those doors? For all I knew there was some kind of fire-breathing dragon. After all, anything can happen in a dream world. And why was she not allowed to go in? Was this some place meant only for me? Now that was a daunting thought. Gathering what courage I had, I wiped my hands on my dress and pulled the door open.

CHAPTER FOUR

NOTHING, AND I MEAN NOTHING, could have prepared me for what I saw. The room I'd just entered was *huge*. The ceiling was three stories high, groin vaulted. The spines of the vaulting buttressed out into separate chambers of space. They sectioned off what seemed like hundreds of bookshelves filling the room. They also separated the room adjoining that, and the one thereafter. I could see the other rooms through the wide arched doorways in-between them. You could fit half of my hometown in those three rooms, I was sure. And that was saying something.

All my senses clicked to high power as the doors closed behind me. I felt like I'd been shut in a tomb or some kind of mausoleum. The sound of those doors closing had been so foreboding, so final. An edge of uneasiness lined my stomach. Anxiety pounded with every heartbeat. I almost wanted to say, "What? No 'don't go to the mountains' today?" I felt ridiculous. It annoyed me.

Mom had always told me I had a sense of telling the future. I sensed things others didn't, and often felt when things were going to happen. That's why she understood about the Voice. It was a warning. But why hadn't she understood about it this morning? Was it this morning, or some other morning? I wasn't sure. But I did feel like something big was happening right now. My stomach was in knots.

I tried to calm my racing heart by breathing in. Or trying to. My breath caught in my throat. I couldn't see anyone. Well, there were a few people who I guessed were servants, but no one besides them. They ignored me anyway.

I focused on one of the shelves, trying to figure out the layout of this place. It wasn't like I had anything else to do. There were several alcoves where couches sat in horseshoe shapes. A large fireplace, larger than the one in my room, completed one of these horseshoe arrangements. I could feel its heat even though I was more than a dozen yards from it. Ten or fifteen people could fit inside that hearth without touching. They could probably even dance in there.

My hand brushed over several volumes of books. They were all bound like the ones in my room. I started to walk down the rows of shelves, trying to find a familiar title among all the strange ones. It gave me something to do, something to focus on besides the fear.

I saw Chaucer's *Canterbury Tales*, Spencer's *Fairy Queen*. They were set among hundreds of other books I didn't know existed in print. Boethius' *Consolation of Philosophy* and *Lai d'Orfey*. This was crazy. *Lai d'Orfey* didn't exist anymore. There were no remaining copies. I found a book by John Steinbeck.

Several men in dark green uniforms dusted books a row down. Their footsteps echoed on the polished marble floor. The telltale click followed a slight squish of something like rubber soles, but not quite the same. I started down a different row so I wouldn't bother them. I let my fingertips trace the edges of the various books, all that same hardbound material as those in the bedroom I'd woken up in. I inspected my fingers. No dust. Those guys were really good at their jobs.

My skin tingled with some kind of feeling I couldn't describe and I stopped in my tracks. I heard someone breathing behind me. If it weren't so quiet, I wouldn't have heard that sound. The hair raised on the back of my neck. I could have sworn no one was close to me.

"Do not turn around. I do not wish to frighten you." The voice was definitely masculine.

I turned around anyway, expecting to see someone, anyone. I saw nothing, nothing but bookshelves with more books. "Where are you? Who are you?"

I leaned against the nearest shelf, glad it was sturdy, as unmovable as a mountain. I hoped I wasn't too obvious about doing it. My heart was pounding so fast now that it made breathing difficult and I felt somewhat dizzy because of it.

"Look down, near the end of this shelf. You will see my shadow. Don't be afraid." His voice was gentle, maybe a tenor. His words were careful, caressing. Not trusting that voice was hard. It was like a gently flowing stream filled with sunlight.

I did as he asked and almost stepped back in shock, though I controlled myself. There it was all right. And if my mind was processing things right, he should have been standing in front of me, no more than a foot away. The space was empty. I took a deliberate step back, feeling suddenly claustrophobic, even though I couldn't see anything.

"How? Why?" I stuttered. "Are you a ghost? Or are you playing games with me? If you are, I'm not in the mood."

"No, Kas." I heard a sigh in his voice and was tempted to feel pity for him. "I am the chosen Master of this place and you are a newcomer, not yet accustomed to the way things work here. The Waymeet of Worlds is an odd sort of place. It is not anywhere but everywhere all at once, even if I am not."

His voice held a trace of irony in it I didn't understand. "You can hear me and see my shadow because you were allowed to come here. But you will not see my true form until you discover something you have known all along. Unfortunately, I cannot tell you what that is. You must discover this on your own."

"What kind of nonsense is that? Discover something I've known all along?" I snorted, which was better than the alternative of screaming. There was enough presence of mind left me to wonder if this wasn't some prank after all. It had to be a crock, some kind of joke. Puleeze. I wouldn't let it scare me anymore.

"I remember the first step you took when you were only so tall." The shadow of his hand moved to try and show some approximation of height but it wasn't as effective as it might have been if I could see him.

"What are you, some kind of ghost stalker or something?" My sarcasm didn't seem to make a dent.

"No, but I do know all about you," he continued, almost like he was remembering something, something amusing. "I've watched you grow up and I've seen you grow old. I know you have never cared for anyone the way I care about you. I know that you have always felt out of place. Even your family always considered you to be the odd child. You were always off in some other world, some other fantasy. And they don't seem to understand any of it."

If he was trying to intimidate me I wouldn't let it work. "I'm not old! I'm seventeen, for crying out loud! And how could you know all about me if you've never even met me before? Tell me that."

I edged back a little more, trying to imagine what he had to look like. I pictured someone with a wart and haggard face, even if the voice was soft. It made it easier to not like him. And by avoiding the thought that he might be some kind of monster, I was able to keep my fear at bay.

"I must warn you there are some things I cannot tell you now, nor may I ever be able to. You must realize this if nothing else."

"Why? Why must I 'realize this'?" I held my hands up in mock quotation marks. "Why do I even have to listen to any of this… this…?" Words failed me.

"Kas, you are a long way from Brintley. The moment you set foot on the mountains only one day ago, you set a chain of events into motion. Perhaps your instincts were right in telling you not to come." His voice was filled with remorse. But, for some odd reason, I felt more resentful because of it.

"If you really do know all about me, then you'd know I purposely let Mom make my decision about going. I wasn't about to let a Voice scare me away from seeing my family." I twined my fingers in the folds of my skirt. It was a habit I'd had since I was small, twining my fingers in any cloth I could get my hands on. I liked the feel of the fabric between my fingers. It was a comfort thing.

"Why don't you come and sit down," he invited. "It might make you more comfortable." His shadow started to move toward the large fireplace I'd noticed earlier. I could hear his footsteps on the tiling. I almost thought I felt his hand on my shoulder, turning me around to follow him. But I could have been wrong.

I followed his shadow to one of the alcoves and took a seat on a lavender colored sofa. He must have sat down on the seat opposite me because the cushion settled in an odd manner. His shadow crossed its legs. I was tempted to be fascinated but kept myself from that by glaring. "I just want to know what's going on," I said.

"As I told you, there are some things I cannot explain. There are some things I do not know myself. If I did, you can rest assured I would tell you. But you do need to know that I am the one who had you brought here. I called you from your world. Because it is time--"

"Time for what?" I interrupted him.

"If you would let me finish you might hear what you want or need to hear." I was satisfied to hear a touch of impatience or perhaps anger in his voice, though I might have just imagined it.

I watched with fascination and frustration as the cushion rumpled itself about. It was all so bizarre and yet my brain seemed to be taking it all in calmly and rationally, like this were all commonplace. I knew better. This wasn't natural at all. This was Todorov's uncanny and marvelous. These were terms and ideas I'd never thought I'd use outside of my literature classes in college.

"It is time for you to discover who you are, Kas. You are not who you think you are. You have a different destiny than what your parents thought. If you didn't, you wouldn't be here." His tone was earnest, almost serious. Or was I just trying to make it into something it wasn't?

He lies. Believe nothing he says.

It was my Voice, the same that had warned me about going to the mountains. What was it doing here now?

He will destroy you if he can.

How dare it come back now when it had abandoned me in the woods?

"You have nothing to fear from me. I only want to help you," the invisible man implored.

I blinked a few times. I could feel the start of several tears leaking at the corner of my eyes. At least I hoped they were tears, even if they were angry ones. "Help me?" I was so upset that my voice squeaked.

"Yes. I want to help you become who you were meant to be, to see your full potential. It is time you learned the truth."

He lies. Do not listen to him.

I arched back my neck and stared at the ceiling, silently asking, why me? Was I going mad? The quiet tenor of this invisible man sounded strange with the deeper baritone of the Voice in the background.

"I can protect you."

From what, I wondered. From myself? From you? From my Voice? Why did I need protection in the first place? Why was I here? Why did he call me here? Or was he lying about that too?

You see? He causes only confusion. Listen to me. I will help you escape him. He doesn't want to help you. He will only use you.

I shuddered. I felt like I was trapped between two panes of glass with two different voices speaking at me all at the same time. I covered my ears with my hands. Their words jumbled together, one hissing like a snake, the other using the soft tones of imploring.

Their voices made my brain buzz inside and out. I didn't know how much more I could take. Their voices combined into a single, yet multi-harmony hiss of words, lisps, and snarls. I felt like I was slipping around inside my skin, sloshing around my bones, and slowly draining into a whirlpool between my eyes.

"Stop it!" I had no idea how loud I'd said those two words, but apparently it wasn't loud enough.

He will only destroy you. He cares nothing for you. Trust me. Have I led you wrong yet?

I could see the cushions opposite me tilting forward, along with the Master's shadow. "You are more than what you have become. At least listen to what I have to say." His voice was pleading with me.

I had no idea how long they'd both been talking to me, confusing me. It might have only been a moment. It could have been years. I couldn't tell.

"Shut up!" I stood, flinging my arms out as if to ward off an attacker. "This is wrong! All wrong!" I ran for the door, tripping over my dress on the way. I continued to slosh inside my skin, which didn't make things any easier. I imagined that this must be what it felt like to be drunk. I didn't like it.

"Kas!" I almost felt him reaching out a hand to stop me.

Yes, run Little One. Flee before him. He will only destroy you.

I could hear laughter in my head, or was it only my imagination? It didn't matter.

Run, little one. He will only devour you like a wild dog.

"No!" I got up and ran past startled servants. I could have sworn they were ravenous wolves only a moment before. The doors leading from the library stood wide open and I dashed through them. Part of me had enough sense to wonder why they were open since they'd been closed when I'd come in. I knocked Jenny over on my way out but I didn't really care. My feet took me down the opposite end of the hall, bare feet on carpet. I didn't even have time to apologize before I was out of sight.

I threw open a door, it didn't matter which one, and let it slam shut behind me. At least I think I did. It seemed to me that my body split in two. One part continued down the hall, towards some stairs heading down, and one entering the strange room I was in now. I didn't care where I was so long as both the Master and the Voice couldn't follow me. I collapsed onto the first piece of furniture I could find, a large pouf of some sort, like a giant cupcake turned into a chair.

I pounded on the fabric, wishing the tears would come. I tried to will my being to settle back around my bones. But my eyes remained dry and my innards did not settle. Why me? Why was this happening to me? Why couldn't it be someone else? I asked myself these questions over and over. This couldn't be a dream, unless it was a nightmare.

Eventually, someone found me and returned me to my room. I didn't pay any more attention to my surroundings than I had the furnishings of the room I'd tried to cry in. My feet felt like lead. I was tired, so tired.

CHAPTER FIVE

SOMEONE LED ME DOWN A vast hallway. The shadows fell in an odd manner. My mind refused to understand why. Dark shapes seemed to lurk in the darker corners, waiting to lunge out at me. But someone was walking by my side, keeping them at bay. I couldn't see who it was. It was almost as if my eyes were closed and refused to open.

We approached a door that looked familiar, the silver handle whispering that this was my room. Instead of opening it, my escort opened another door and led me into a new room. He melted into the shadows so completely I couldn't help but wonder if he'd really been there at all or if I'd just dreamed him. Like everything else. It had to be a dream. There was no other explanation.

This new room was smaller than the other and was warm. Steam rose from the floor, which was cobalt blue. A large old-fashioned porcelain bathtub stood in the middle of tiles, towels, and soap. It sat up on clawed feet, keeping it from settling into the floor. Two maids waited beside it. Neither of them was Jenny.

One walked forward with a simple grace and started to remove my clothes. I was almost too tired to register that she'd almost completely taken off my dress and was now working on the petticoat underneath it. She had just started to remove that when my brain woke up enough to realize my danger and I moved out of her reach.

"What do you think you're doing!?" I backed away even more so neither maid could spring anything on me. I felt like a trapped animal. Where was Jenny? My hair brushed against my waist. I could feel it through the thin undershirt. Or did they call it a shift?

"Please, lady." The maids looked flustered and confused all at the same go, if that's possible. "You do not wish to bathe? We only mean to help you."

I was stared at in such a manner that I felt I had somehow offended them; then a reference from a book I once read came back to me. I remembered enough about the story to realize this was a reenactment of the bathing scene. It was about a servant turned royalty, only to learn she wasn't allowed to do anything by herself.

I glanced at them. They couldn't possibly mean to--No way. They gestured towards the tub, confirming my fears. I groaned as I stared at them. I tried to gather the courage to confront them on the subject but my efforts were in vain. Perhaps my resolve had continued on down the hallway and stairs I'd seen when my soul split itself in two.

"I like taking my baths alone," I said, trying to be forceful. I always delighted in my privacy. How could I make them understand? There just didn't seem to be a way, without offending them that is. Or burning down the castle. Was it a castle? And did I even care? The rules must be different here, just like in that story reference I'd remembered. I ended up submitting myself to their care.

But I didn't like it. I was just too tired to argue.

It was strange to have someone else wash my back and hair. I couldn't help but feel embarrassed. This was my body after all. Why didn't they have showers? That was all I wanted right now. I would have been more content to wake up from this mad circus but that didn't seem likely to happen any time soon. This place was by far the most backwards I'd ever seen. What a nightmare.

I can make this all go away. I can spare you from this dream. Trust me.

I rolled my eyes at the Voice. "You're the one who got me into this mess," I told it. I sulked, folding my arms until the ordeal was over. Why did I have to be so obstinate?

When I was finally deemed clean, the maids returned to my original room. This was after they'd slipped me into a light robe and wound a towel around my damp hair. Even then I wasn't allowed my privacy. I had to endure while they fussed over my hair, combing out the tangles and braiding it. Why did I insist on having it long? Then I had to wait while they dressed me in a silky nightgown, like one would a doll. I was the plaything of dreams.

Finally, I was left alone, staring into the fire. I didn't know whether to rampage in a fit, cry, or just sit there forever. I allowed myself to wallow in desolation. I was alone, and, as far as I knew, a million miles away from my family. They must be worried sick. I could just imagine them searching for me but finding nothing.

Or, maybe, I was in the hospital and this was all just a dream, a fantasy induced by drugs or a coma. I had hit my head rather hard when I fell. Everything else seemed like a dream already anyway.

A dream that we can make go away if you would only let us.

The tiredness slipped from my bones and I found myself becoming angry. "Yeah right, just like you were able to keep me from this mess. I thought you said you'd protect me."

I will. You have only to let us.

What was this nonsense? If only I would let *them*? I shivered. My Voice had lied to me too? There was more than one of them? What other delightful surprises were in store for me? I was really some space alien? Or maybe I was just some figment of some psycho's imagination?

At this point, I wasn't sure if anything would surprise me anymore. But even if that prospect was true, I was still myself in my own eyes, somehow the key player in this situation that was out of control. I could take control, or at least that's what I told myself. I would not be manipulated anymore.

"I'm not taking any more of this," I stated. "I'm getting out of here." I grabbed the robe the maids had left me and put it on as I strode out the door, heading towards some stairs I somehow knew were there. Were they the same ones I'd seen some image of myself running down earlier? Weren't they on the other side of this building?

The maids must have seen my flight, or the madness of desperate resolve in my eyes. Maybe that's why they tried to stop me. Or, maybe, I was their prisoner and they didn't want me to escape. I paid no attention except to start running.

I didn't like what was going on. I realized I didn't have any control and I wanted out of all it. I didn't even have any control over hearing my little Voice. Or was it Voices? And I definitely didn't have any control over anything else. It was about time I took the reins.

There had to be a million stairs to the main floor, not to mention the winding corridors. I felt like I'd raced down thousands of them. They seemed to be unending. Finally, I reached the bottom flight, which opened up into the main hall. My feet hit the bottom stair with a shock, as if they couldn't believe they'd reached the end.

A set of large double doors beckoned to me from across the way. Servants, footmen, maids, you name it, were everywhere. It looked like an ant farm. Some called out to me to stop. Others tried to block my path. They only added to my frenzied state. They had to be in on this. Every last one of them.

Something was wrong with my world and I only wanted to escape from it. I didn't care if it was snowing outside and my feet were bare, which turned out to be the case. Didn't I put slippers on when I was upstairs? I couldn't remember.

I reached the doors and, with an effort, pulled them open. I was struck by a sudden blast of cold air. Hard snow lashed at my face but I was beyond caring, even though my brain told me that it shouldn't be snowing this early on in the year.

There was something wrong with this thought though. I knew it had been snowing. I had seen it from my window only that morning. But was it still morning? What was going on? Why did my world feel so upside down?

I ran on outside, not daring to look behind me for fear of seeing some creature like the Beast from my fantasies. I was a panic driven animal trying to escape capture. Or worse.

I turned around and the half-light of evening surrounded me. Everything else faded to dark mist, even the light that had spilled out from the open doorway. It was almost as if it had never existed.

Out of the corner of my eye, I could see the horse gaining on me all over again. But this time I could see his rider's face. It was a hideous mask of hate, something you'd expect to find on the Headless Horseman from Sleepy Hollow. Flaming eyes, evil but insane grin, wild hair.

And then my mind reeled. *Again?* Was there any sanity to all this? Was this a recurring dream? The same nightmare I'd had my entire life? I almost faltered in my steps but caught myself before I twisted an ankle. That wasn't supposed to happen yet.

I turned back towards the rose bushes I somehow knew were coming soon. My feet were already numb from the cold ground. I tried to run but everything was going in slow motion. I felt like I was running through jello or some thick liquid. Maybe it was pudding. Everything was blurred at the edges like a fast-motion scene played at half speed.

Snow was falling down all around us, the horseman and me. The snow disappeared under our feet, running ahead of us like wind whipped silk. It was the only thing that didn't seem to be moving in slow motion.

I reached the rose bushes and they reached out for me, lifting their long branches to grab my legs with gnarled hands. One grabbed my arm and tore into the flesh. I screamed but no sound came from my mouth. Only the feeling of choking on air.

Then I was falling, falling in a twisting motion. One ankle was trapped between branch and soil so that I, once again, saw the horseman come swooping down at me. His hot breath baked my throbbing skin into dust. He reached down from the saddle with an arm made of flame and claws of steel.

I sucked in a lungful of air, the dark-red flames burning down into my lungs. I was screaming again, screaming in silence as I stared with eyes that now refused to focus.

I felt cloth in my clenched fists. *"It is not too late, Kas. Let me help you."*

He reached for me and pulled me up onto the saddle in front of him. My mind was released from my body. I watched myself bounce against the man. My body flipped to and fro, like a rag doll. My mind was dragged behind like a balloon on a string. Definitely not the most comfortable of sensations.

With the speed of demons, he galloped back towards the castle. Only it wasn't the same castle. It was black, sucking all light out of the air around it. I decided there and then that if this was what my fantasy worlds were really like, I wanted nothing of them.

We passed through a high arching tunnel, vaulted with large cracks of black. Torches burned in sconces set high above our heads. Purple light. On the other side of this tunnel was a circular space of just grass, with no snow to be seen.

Several hooded figures stood in an incomplete circle. They were waiting for me. Their robes were dark brown, so dark they were almost black. Except they weren't. They looked poisonous green in the purple light.

The rider checked the horse to a walk as we entered the circle of waiting men. He let out a phrase of some awful sounding language and handed my body down to one of the hooded men. My mind was called back to my body the moment his cold fingers touched my skin. I could almost look at his face but his hood was too low to see any detail.

I knew him somehow, even without seeing his face, and that idea was disconcerting to say the least. He set me on the ground, my head tilted up to look at the other hooded men who had crowded in around me.

The horseman dismounted from his horse and stepped forward. His movement completed the circle surrounding me. The others held me in a vice grip so I couldn't move. My body was trembling so much I couldn't understand how they were able to hold my shoulders so still. His step was full of purpose and I didn't like the calculated stride as he entered the circle. He knelt down in front of me and pulled back his hood. I shrank back inside myself at the sight.

I wanted to scream. I cried to scream, tears rolling down my cheeks, tears that weren't there. Tears that would not or could not blur out my returned vision, could not or would not hide that face from my sight.

The one who held my shoulders tightened his grip and I fought. I lashed out, trying to break free. My body rocked and I heard the snap of limbs as I lunged forward.

And…

I was sitting up in bed, sweat rolling down my face. My chest was heaving. The movement was too fast to catch a decent breath. I was in the same bedroom as before. The hooded men weren't there, as if they'd never existed. Except in my mind. I couldn't see them, even when I turned wildly from side to side, looking.

Jenny was sitting on the edge of the bed, holding my hand. She squeezed and squeezed until my hand felt like melting butter. Fear was etched in her eyes. She dropped my hand as I looked at her. I had no idea what kind of expression I had on my face.

"You were screaming," she said, backing away from me. "You were screaming." There were tears running down her face, just as there was sweat running down mine. My mind refused to understand what she was saying.

I leaned forward, stretching my arms out in front of me and idly noticed they were scratched. Dark scabs ran up and down them in the same pattern from my dream. It was only a dream, I told myself. It had to have been only a dream. Someone was playing with my head.

My heart started to beat normally after the third time I told myself it hadn't been real. It wasn't real. I was so exhausted I fell into a dreamless sleep.

CHAPTER SIX

A FIRE CRACKLED TO ITSELF in the fireplace the next morning. The curtains were pulled away from every window, allowing the morning light to flood into the room. A tray lay on a nearby table, close to the one with the hairbrushes. It was laden with fresh fruit and a bowl of cream. There was even a glass of fresh squeezed orange juice.

Breakfast, I thought. No toast. My stomach growled, reminding me I hadn't eaten for a while. I just had no idea how long ago my last meal was. Bu I didn't want to leave my warm bed, even though my stomach was winning that battle, complete with loud complaints. Life isn't fair!

A thought came to me as I contemplated leaving my warm nest. Curious, I looked at my arms. The scratches from my dreams were still there. If my rose scratches were real, had my ankle been injured too? I had to find out.

Carefully, I slid my left foot, the unharmed one, out from under the covers, and put it on the floor. It felt all right. So far so good, I told myself, gearing up to move the other one. I slid my right foot to join it and let it press against the carpet. Sharp pain shot up my leg and I quickly took the weight off. Had I really twisted it that much in the thorns?

After a minute or so I figured it wouldn't hurt to try again. Why did I have to be so stubborn? Clenching my teeth in wary anticipation, I put my foot back on the ground and stepped on it. Hard. I fell to the floor, making a sound like some drowning animal.

I was sure that if it had not been broken before, it sure as anything was now. At least I knew this part couldn't be a dream. I'd never felt pain in a dream before, even if I had dreamed about being gored by a wild animal.

"Oh Miss!" Jenny was by my side before I could so much as blink. I hadn't known she was still in the room. Her eyes were full of concern as she helped me into a nearby chair. "Does it hurt?" She traced a finger over the swollen appendage. "Don't move. I'll summon the doctor."

I watched her run through the doorway and down the hall. She didn't even wait for my answer but I didn't mind too much. I'd have fired off some snide comment if she'd stayed anyway. Or would I have? I wasn't sure. The pain was excruciating.

I'm sure my ankle had swollen to twice its original size and was turning an angry red. I wondered why it hadn't been wrapped up the night before. But it had only been a dream. Just a dream. Right? What was going on? My mind refused to focus.

———

Suddenly, I was crying on the pouf, crying dry tears in that one room. My mind was a magnet, a multi-screen TV with thousands of channels flipping on and off to various scenes and images. Some of those images I knew I had seen before. Parts of movies. Memories. Dreams. They were all there, all calling to me, reaching out to me. There were so many of them.

My brain refused to work the way it should. I was processing information way beyond what I was capable of putting into words. And that honestly scared the tar out of me.

"It is a gift, a gift you have possessed from birth. You need only learn to harness it."

This voice was feminine. I hadn't heard this voice before, not that I knew of at any rate. But I liked it. It was gentle, caressing like a dove. I wanted to hear that voice more than anything else in the world. It was a part of me but not a part of me.

"You have the strength to get there, Kas. I know you do. Look inside yourself."

My mind and my thoughts were not my own. I was being lifted up, held by some invisible blanket of love so pure that I couldn't comprehend it. Thousands of rays of light shattered inside my head, forming rainbows of colors so brilliant I cried out.

"My lady!" Someone was calling me, calling me away from this love, this pure love that wrapped around my soul. I didn't want to leave it, but someone was calling.

It was morning and I was lying on my bed in the castle. Jenny was calling me to wake up. I opened my eyes and smiled. "Jenny. I didn't hear you come in. How long have I been asleep?"

"Not long, my lady. Not long at all." Jenny smiled down at me. "Milord sent you these." She brought over a vase of wild flowers and I buried my nose in their scent.

"Come back, Kas. You can't escape everything that easily. You must learn from the experiences you are trying to avoid. You cannot

jump to the future. Not yet. You must deal with the here and now."
The woman's voice was soothing, even though I didn't like what she had to say.

The hooded rider. I could see him clearly. My body stiffened at the recollection. I could see his eyes glaring at me again through the pain. I had to clench my teeth to not cry out. Why must I do this? Why couldn't I go ahead, to Jenny and the wild flowers that Milord had brought me? Already that existence was starting to fade from my mind.

Who was Milord? My lack of control over my memories made me angry. Everything was slipping away, like water draining from a tub.

After who knew how long, Jenny returned with an elderly man. He carried a bag that almost looked like the old doctor bags in TV shows. It was tooled from some strange colored leather. And it was purple.

His clothes were not from any style I recognized either. It was nothing like what my brothers would wear. The majority of his outfit was some kind of tailored trench coat with renaissance trousers and tunic underneath it. I didn't like his expression. It reminded me too much of a class bully.

He took one look at my ankle and sighed. "You should not have put weight on it for at least four weeks," he told me.

"Thanks for the info, Doc," I retorted. "Had I known that sooner I wouldn't have tried to kill myself before breakfast. I would have waited until after."

He chose to ignore my sarcasm. Instead of returning a retort, he turned his back to fiddle around in his bag. When he turned back around, he held a bottle of dark liquid and a goblet. He filled the cup with the stuff and handed it to me. "Drink it." It was not a request.

I took the cup with misgivings. "What is it?" I asked and swirled the contents around. I doubted I could trust him. He grunted something about it being for the pain. I eyed it with suspicion and took one sip, only to spit it out. "What is this?" I demanded. "It tastes awful! It's worse than dreaming I've swallowed fire!"

"Brandy," he barked. "What did you expect? Lemon juice?" He looked exasperated. "I'm not prone to dispensing anything else to someone in your position or with your attitude."

"Brandy?" I squeaked. "You dare give me brandy?" I threw the cup to the floor, spilling the foul drink and breaking the glass. Jenny ran for a towel. "If you value your life, you'll keep that filthy stuff away from me!"

"You know, *girl*, I'm not accustomed to being accosted in such a manner," he warned. "You should be grateful I offered you anything at all. You will drink brandy for the pain or you will do without."

"I haven't before this and don't intend to start drinking just to relieve pain," I retorted. "So why don't you get your ugly face and backhanded medicine away from me. If I never see you again I will be happier for it!" I picked up a brush from the nearby table and threw it at him when he looked inclined to stay.

"Get out!" I felt like throwing out a few unladylike words with the brush but didn't on general principle. I don't think Jenny could have handled hearing them. She seemed the sensitive type and I didn't want to press it.

He snorted. "You can banish me for now, little child. The Master will not be happy, I can promise you."

Oh, now he was attacking my height, something I'd always been sensitive about. Everyone at work always called me shorty. I didn't like it anymore than they liked it when I told them what I really thought about them and their own shortcomings. "Out!" I picked up another brush and chucked it. He finally left after I'd thrown several more objects.

Jenny looked appalled and shocked, as I thought she might. It's a good thing she didn't know what thoughts were running around in my head. I ignored her. "Time to put my brain to use," I said and started to tear a strip of cloth from the bottom of my nightgown. At least I could be practical in this mad house.

"Miss!" She put out her hands in protest, though she didn't actually move to stop me.

I waved her off with one hand. I didn't need this right now. "If you want something done right, you've got to do it yourself," I told her.

With my teeth clenched, I felt for broken bones. I couldn't find anything out of place. I just hoped that was a good sign because I didn't have a clue what a broken bone felt like anyway. I knew I should have paid more attention at Youth Camp!

I wrapped the cloth once around my foot, and then started up my ankle, isolating my foot so it wouldn't move too much. At least that's what I hoped. I had to tear off another strip to finish the job. At least the nightgown still reached past my knees; not that modesty was an issue at the moment.

The good thing, for Jenny's sake, was I had calmed down enough that I didn't feel like doing any more damage. She had turned her back during the entire process, wringing her hands. Her apron was getting really wrinkled.

"Jenny, I don't think I can manage much right now. Do you think you could find me something to keep me from going insane?" I asked. Not that I was sure I wasn't already insane. Ron lingered not too far away in my thoughts. I could imagine the smug smile on his face if he ever found out about this.

"Of course, Miss." She curtsied, suddenly being all professional. I stopped her with a gesture.

"Oh, one more thing. Stop calling me miss. I have a name. It's Kas, Kas Lee Stanship. I'd prefer it if you'd call me that, okay?"

She nodded. "Yes Mi--Kas." She turned away from me and left. I hoped she was finding something to occupy my time. My current situation didn't exactly thrill me. I just hoped whatever she found wasn't needlework.

⌇

It wasn't needlework, but some might have considered it related. It was a set of crochet hooks and thin yarn. I rolled my eyes. This wouldn't work. Handicrafts weren't my thing. Not by a long shot. I'd never been good at manipulating those kinds of things.

I drilled my fingers on my forehead, my chin resting in the palm of my left hand. "This isn't exactly what I had in mind, you know," I commented. "Needlework is one thing but crochet? I'd rather think. Granted, I'm still trying to puzzle this whole thing out you know. It's all so bizarre. It can't be happening. Why, it's any girl's dream come true, landing in some story, right? But which story? And what if I don't want to be in this story? What then? Or do I have a choice?"

Was I trying to figure this insane asylum out? Joy. I wanted to kick myself, not that that would have helped matters, or improve my humor, because it wouldn't.

A knock came at the door, interrupting my train of thought. Jenny answered it and was engaged for several minutes by someone I couldn't see. Upon finishing her conversation, she returned to my side.

"My lady, Kas, you must get dressed. The Master wishes to see you in the library." I could almost see her heart fluttering through her little green dress. I was grateful she didn't start wringing her hands again. That would have been overkill.

I nodded. Fine. I would play along. For now. "So, suggestions for what I should wear? I'm not all into the dress thing but I guess you guys don't make anything but dresses for women."

Jenny shook her head. "No, only dresses for the women. At least as far as I know."

I sighed. "All right. Pick out a dress, so long as it isn't fancy. I'd rather have a pair of trousers or something though. Let's just get this over with." I tugged at my tangled hair and wondered whether I was insane or not. I'd just used the word 'trousers' after all.

Jenny called a manservant to carry me to the library after she'd finally managed to untangle my hair. This time I paid more attention to my surroundings. I was sure that I was no longer dreaming and felt a desire to look around, not that I saw all that much. I mean how much can you see when someone is carrying you? I did my best.

We passed a lot of hallways decorated with suits of armor and paintings. There were hundreds of portraits, just like there were hundreds of doors that opened up on the left and right. I didn't see the Robin Hood portrait. It was entirely possible we'd taken a different route than last time. I think I saw an analogue clock through one of those doorways, though I couldn't be sure.

I think I thought about it too much because my head was whirling in confusion. Modern and past things all under one roof. What an interesting thought. Was this some kind of museum? Couldn't be.

Then I remembered something else from that bathroom that I had taken for granted. It had a real toilet in it. There were no chamber pots here, but why was everything else so old-fashioned? I puzzled over this until we finally reached the set of high double doors leading to the library.

Another man opened the doors for us. I could only see a few shelves full of books as I was carried in. The manservant moved towards one of the many alcoves I'd noticed earlier. Once there, he set me on a cushioned chair of deep-red velvet, facing the blazing fireplace. And I mean blazing. That thing warmed me up in record time, probably making my face flush red from the heat.

Large windows allowed light to filter through the room. I turned my head to look behind me but couldn't see many of the shelves from my perch. My unbandaged foot felt the heat from the fire. I'd forgotten to put on socks.

———

All my senses stepped up a notch with the shutting of the door. An edge of uneasiness lined my stomach. Anxiety pounded with every heartbeat. Would the Voice return? Was this all just an endless cycle? Movies where a character was doomed to repeat a single day ran through my head. My stomach was in knots and I regretted breakfast.

I focused on the mantel-piece, looking at the delicate scrollwork of the carved flourishes. They reminded me of paisleys. What a design. The person who created them should have been shot.

"Kas."

It was him. The Master of this place. I felt a puff of air on my neck. I turned my head to try and glimpse whoever was there. The room seemed empty, just like last time. "Hello?"

"Forgive me, Kas." I could hear the rustle of his clothes. And the note of apology in his voice.

"For what?" I wasn't prepared for more surprises. I tried to crane my neck around again. I still couldn't see whoever was talking. Then I remembered his words from before. Of course I couldn't see him. How silly of me.

"That won't do you any good, Kas. Even if I wished it, you would not be able to see me, no matter how hard you crane your neck. It will only be uncomfortable for you."

"Kinda figured that one out on my own." The words escaped my lips before I could even think about what I was saying. It sounded so childish.

He didn't make an answer. Despite that, I knew he had come around and was sitting on the chair opposite me.

Unless someone had managed to make the cushions look like they were occupied that is.

"Who are you? What do you want with me? Why are you holding me here?" I balled up my hands into fists, lost in the folds of my dress. It gave me something to do. "Why did you take me away from my family?"

"You hate me then," he stated calmly.

"You don't give me any reason to like you, but I don't hate you. I don't think I'm capable of hate." My voice betrayed me with the venom of anger. I could imagine him nodding his head knowingly.

"I set some things in motion that made sure you would come. I did not have a choice in the matter. And since then, you have experienced more than I intended for you to. This place… It has a way of doing that. It crawls around and playing with your abilities." His shadow gestured to encompass the room.

"So you, or this place, has been manipulating me from the beginning." No questions here, just outright bluntness.

"Yes." There was my answer, plain and straight out. Not that I'd expected anything else, because I hadn't. "But I could do nothing to you directly. You are who you are. Yet, I did help you on the path here," he continued.

True confessions from a possessed mind. I felt like some lab experiment of Ron's. Or maybe like I was in one of those mystery movies that always gave me the creeps. "So," I started, "where, exactly, is here? I only know what you've told me. Waymeet of Worlds and all that."

"I don't expect you to understand. You never seemed particularly interested in science. If you like, you can say you are still in the mountains. And you are still in reality, but your Old World is more like a shadow now."

"What?" I wanted to blink out my confusion but my eyes didn't want to cooperate. I felt woozy. "Oh, so that's it, is it? I'm not smart enough to get it? Look here, I can understand anything you send my way. What's this about my home being a mere shadow?"

"It is unfortunate that I do not have time to go into any further detail. There are other things I must attend to." I noticed the cushions on his chair returned to their usual height. Had he stood? I wasn't sure. I didn't hear any footsteps. Or fabric rustling.

"Let me guess, more fair maidens you've captured, right? Or were you going to go and apologize to my family for taking me away from them?" I felt dizzy all the sudden. What was wrong with me?

"My business is not yours to know. This only will I tell you, I leave you in good hands, even if they are somewhat talkative." His voice started to recede. It was possible he hadn't even turned a hair at my jibe. Too bad shadows were insubstantial. If I'd had a brush I'd be tempted to throw it and hope it made contact.

"Now wait just a minute!" I wanted to call him moron so badly it hurt, even if it was juvenile. But why risk the wrath of someone determined to thwart my every question? There was one question I really did want answered though.

"Can't you at least indulge me in one simple request? I don't even know your name. In case you forgot, you never told me. What do I call you? Beast?" I felt his eyes on the back of my scalp. At least I think I did. I wanted to ask him more questions, but didn't want to press my luck.

He thought for a moment. I was almost afraid he'd left without answering, but then he spoke again. His voice was so quiet I wasn't quite sure I'd heard right. "Call me . . . Call me Milord."

I could imagine him turning to go. His footsteps were certainly loud enough. "Rest assured that I will see to your welfare often. I am satisfied. You may leave."

I was put out, like the flame of a candle quickly snuffed. "But, Milord! Are you blind as well as bodiless? I'm not exactly in the best of circumstances for just leaving or doing anything!" My words echoed without an answer. He was gone. "You can't do this! I have a job!"

CHAPTER SEVEN

IT SNOWED FOR THE REST of the afternoon. I stayed in my room, hiding in the shadows. The only source of light came from the flames in the fireplace. I wasn't hungry when lunch came. I picked at my food, not tasting it. I would have paced had it not been for my ankle.

Jenny stayed with me almost every minute. I wished she'd just leave me alone. Her presence only made me more aware of my imprisonment. Especially since she kept pacing, reminding me that I couldn't. I know it wasn't necessary a willful thing, but I couldn't help but feel it.

I wondered what Milord was doing. Was he watching from some distance? Was he off doing some unknown errand, or was he just pulling my chain the entire time? Was it even okay for me to think something like that? Oh well. So much for my reputation.

He said he'd known me all my life. Was he trying to give me what I thought I wanted? Why did I have to be so adamant about my fairy tales? They were nothing like what I was experiencing. Or were they? Things always seem different when you're living them. You can look back at some things and laugh, but I don't think this would be one of those times. I'd have given almost anything for some modern technology, besides the toilet.

"Isn't there something I can do? Isn't there a computer? A T.V.? A gaming system? Anything?" I was desperate. If all this doesn't kill me, it will drive me to insanity. I wished I'd paid more attention to Ron and his psychobabble. I could've probably diagnosed myself with schizophrenia or Multiple Personality Disorder by now.

Jenny looked on without comment. She didn't seem to have a clue. And to think I wanted to go back to the "good old days". I was so bored I found myself counting things in the room. There were twelve hairbrushes, five combs, and hundreds of different ribbons and bangles. Someone had put the brushes back on the table.

I counted five chairs in various locations, one near the bed, one near the fire, two by the doors, and one rocking chair by the window. I think someone moved it away from the fireplace when I wasn't looking. There was also the only hardwood desk near the far wall.

I stared at the carpet, a deep blue color with greenish blotches every few inches. Those stupid cabbages. It was short carpet and didn't cover the floor in front of the fireplace. The tiles there were in five rows with ten columns. Each tile was a foot square. The tiles were white with a cream colored pattern of paisleys. What was with all the paisleys anyway?

The walls were hardwood, cherry stained I think. A bookshelf sat against one wall near the fireplace. There were perhaps two-dozen books on the thing but I couldn't see anything that looked interesting to read. And, of course, I was being redundant.

See what boredom does to you? But books. That got my brain working. If only I had a good book to escape into. And there was no way I was going to play invalid if I could help it. I liked my independence too much. It was a trait that had annoyed Mom, and my siblings, to no end.

"Jenny," I called out, "could you find me a stiff pair of boots and a walking stick? I want to get up and about." I stared at the fireplace, watching the flames dance. If I wasn't careful, I'd fall asleep in my chair.

Jenny stood from her embroidery, something she'd picked up after I mentioned gaming systems. "Yes, Miss." She put her sewing on the table.

"Kas," I said without turning.

"Kas," she corrected herself and curtsied. I didn't even need to see her to know she'd done that. I waited for her to leave before turning back around.

I limped over to the window and peered past the curtains. The snow was falling in large flakes. I'd never seen flakes so large before. I pressed my forehead against the thick glass and closed my eyes. I could will the pain away if I tried. I'd done it before.

I'd once fallen off a piano bench when I was little and had knocked the wind out of my lungs. It hurt but I didn't complain. I just pretended the pain was gone and continued doing whatever I'd set out to do. After I'd caught my breath again, that is. Just like that incident, I wouldn't let this one get the best of me either. If nothing else, Milord had to know that. I would not let this setback cage me, even if this castle was a prison.

Jenny returned after a while. I didn't have a clue how long she'd been gone. There were no clocks in this room. I'd only seen that one analogue one this morning, though it seemed like an eternity had passed between then and now. She placed the boots by my feet and pulled the rocking chair closer.

I sat down and pulled the first boot on over my left foot. The right one was trickier. I had to loosen the laces a lot before my foot would go in. Jenny watched the entire process in silence. She resisted the urge to help when I cringed with pain. I gave her a look that said, "Stay put". If I hadn't, I'm sure she would have given in. I was determined to do this on my own.

I looked down at the boots with admiration. They were stiff enough to fit my purpose, I hoped. They reached almost up to my knees and seemed to support my ankle perfectly. I tried them out by pacing the room. I still limped a little, but I kind of expected that. "Yes, these work wonderfully," I complimented. The cane she had brought was also a big help. A crutch would have been better, but who was I to complain?

I dismissed her after telling her I didn't want to be disturbed no matter what. I planned to make my way back to the library to find some kind of clue about my captor. He had to have been in the room with me. And if not, he either had tons of technological stuff hidden around, like speakers and cameras, or he had magical powers. I figured he was just good at hiding. Everything else had just been a ruse of sorts. There was no way I was crazy. They were all just playing with my head.

I also decided it wouldn't hurt to see just what exactly this guy had in his library. I might find something interesting. Fairy stories didn't seem to appeal to me at the moment. I wanted something cold. Hard. Something real. I wanted a mystery I could delve into. Anything else I might find on the way would be just as good. Except for a fairy tale.

I encountered no one on my way through the halls. It seemed as though someone was making sure my request to Jenny was fulfilled. I didn't know whether to be thankful or wary. My journey back to the library seemed to take less time than when I had gone there that morning. Maybe it was only because I was beginning to recognize the way. Maybe I found a more direct route. I was just glad things no longer seemed to go in slow motion.

When I passed through the large double-doors, I realized I hadn't caught the actual enormity of the place. The library was spacious, to be sure. Arched doorways connected each of the three rooms. Minus the doors. Books lined the shelves from floor to ceiling. Every title you could think of was there. Every author had at least two books in the assortment, even those authors who I'd thought had written only one. Either that or there were a lot of authors with the same name. I never would have thought that there were so many books in the world.

I wandered down rows of books, past furniture conveniently placed in case someone wanted to sit and rest for a bit. I thought about doing that but decided against it. Instead, I went into the next room. The shelves faced in a different pattern here. They all seemed to face inward in protective walls. It reminded me of a maze. I could see the third room down a clear stretch on one side.

Following through this maze of shelves and novels, I finally made it to the middle of the room where a small table waited. It was made of some hardwood I didn't recognize. The grain was marbled dark and light, carved with care, but well worn. On top of this table was a single book. The hardbound cover was well worn and had no title.

Curious, I opened the cover and thumbed through the yellowing pages. I closed the book in disappointment. All the pages were blank. A book so well used and centrally placed had to have something important inside. Even if only a few words scribbled in haste. It didn't make much sense.

I turned away from the table and looked at the books on the shelf closest to me but felt a prickling against my neck. Someone was watching me, I felt sure of it. I turned around. Only the book was there. Books don't have eyes, I told myself.

I turned back around and the same feeling persisted. What was with this? It had to be coming from the book, unless there were more invisible people hanging around. That would make life more miserable, to be sure. I was done with surprises.

Despite this, I was also curious so I returned to the table and picked up the volume, surprised at its light weight. The volume had at least two hundred thick pages. The strangest thing about it was how familiar it felt in my hand. It almost felt as though I'd owned this particular book since I'd been a small child. But I knew that was ridiculous. I'd grown up in Brintley, not this psychotic nightmare

The desire to cry filled me as I thought of home. What must they be doing right now? I couldn't even imagine. I'd been here for, what… three, maybe four, days? They had to still be looking for me. Too bad they wouldn't find me. Unless I really was in a coma in some hospital.

I closed my eyes and breathed in. There was something wrong with the air. I shivered, the scratches on my skin burning with fire. My ankle throbbed. I reached out a hand for something to steady myself with and felt the solid table under my fingers. I leaned towards that anchor as dizziness filled my senses all over again.

"Please no," I whispered as I sank down to my knees, trying to keep my ankle from twisting further. The cane slipped from my grasp.

I heard faint laughter in my ear. Gleeful. Sadistic. I gasped for breath and my lungs filled with ice. This was worse than what I'd felt at the Sitting Rock back home. This was worse than my half-dream of running from a flaming horseman. It was ten times worse because I couldn't even remember *how* to breathe.

I felt pain running up and down every part of me, inside and out And sick, sick to the core. There was no way someone could feel this bad.

They will destroy you… unless you let me protect you.

But what was attacking me? Or was something attacking me? Was I attacking myself from the inside out?

I had no answers. I didn't know if I could trust anyone else to have them either. The only sure thing was that my world was turning itself inside out. My body felt like it was trying to do the same thing.

I dug my fingernails into the wood surface of the table. I scrunched the rest of me into a fetal position. "Help me!" My voice was lower than a whisper. There wasn't enough air for anything louder. The pain wouldn't allow it anyway. I wasn't sure whom I was asking for help. I don't think it was the Voice. It could have been my mother. I don't know. I just know I had to say it.

I must have blacked out for a moment because the next thing I felt was a cushion underneath me. I was sitting on some kind of couch; my legs drawn up to my chest. And I was shivering.

"Kas," I heard someone say. "Kas?" The voice was gentle but concerned. I thought I felt someone's hand caress my face, feeling my forehead for a fever.

I opened my eyes and looked around. A large fireplace drew my gaze, the fire blazing. I found myself sitting on a red velvet couch.

"Are you all right?"

I blinked and looked around in confusion. I knew that voice. "Milord? Is that you? What's going on?"

"It's all right," his voice soothed. "You fell asleep while we were talking. You must have been dreaming."

"It's so cold," I shivered, my teeth chattering.

I heard footsteps and then felt something being placed around my shoulders. It became visible as soon as it touched my skin. It was a fur coverlet. "I hope this helps," he said. I followed the sound of his footsteps until they stopped at the chair across from me. The cushions settled themselves. He must have sat down again.

"How long have I been out?" I wondered.

"It has been several hours," came his reply. "You fell asleep while I was still talking. I believe the last thing you may have heard was my remark that I had other things to take care of."

I shook my head in confusion. "No, I remember you leaving. You just disappeared, leaving me here. Didn't you?"

"No. I have been with you the entire time. I never left."

"But didn't you tell me I could call you Milord? I remember you telling me that."

"And perhaps I did, in your dreams. Or it was something you heard from Jenny or one of the other servants. That is what some call me. If you wish, you may also call me by that name."

I pressed one hand to my forehead, then ran it through my hair. "This doesn't make sense."

He gave a half-laugh and the cushions rearrange themselves again. I saw an outline of color for a moment before it was gone. I had to blink just to make sure I had my eyes open. The color I'd seen was some sort of green.

The grandfather clock sitting down the hall struck the hour. It was much later than I thought it should be. I dropped my eyes and started picking at one of the long scabs on my arm. It was a bad habit; one Mom had been trying to break me from for years.

"Kas, what have you done to yourself? You're injured."

I felt warm flesh touch my arm as I looked up at his tone. It was unnerving to not see anything more than a shadow cast from the firelight. I pulled my arm back from his probing fingers. I hadn't even heard him walk back over.

"I thought you'd noticed that this morning," I said.

"No, I had not," he confessed. "I admit my mind was not on the present. As I told you, there were other things I had to attend to."

"But you said you'd been here the entire time," I protested.

"My servants came and went while you slept," he reassured me. "But that does not tell me how you procured those wounds."

I looked down, resisting the urge to pick at the healing flesh. "I had a dream last night. At least I think it was a dream," I confessed with some reluctance. Wasn't this all a dream anyway? "I dreamed I tried to run away and a horseman followed and captured me. Trying to escape, I stumbled into some thick bushes and they scratched up my arms and legs." I held out my arms as proof. "I twisted my ankle or broke it. I don't know which for sure. When I woke up, I discovered my scabs were real but I was sure it had all only been a dream."

The cushions next to me pressed flat, as if he was pressing his back against them as he sat back down. I felt warm skin caressing the scabs on my left arm. It felt nice, though I was still surprised he'd chosen to sit this close to me.

I looked down at my feet and back up in surprise. "That's weird," I said.

"What?" His shadow leaned forward. I could feel his body heat press closer to me. It felt odd but comforting at the same time.

"I'm wearing stiff boots. They're the ones Jenny brought me…. But if I fell asleep here, how did…?" I blinked in confusion.

Milord sighed. "I wish I had an answer for you. Some things cannot be explained. Like why you are here, why any of us are here. Some things must be found in their own due time. Until then, it is best to settle down and try to be more careful, even in your dreams. They tend to reflect into reality, especially here."

I raised my eyebrows. "Settle down? You mean accept that I'm here and that I'm not likely to leave any time soon, right? No offense or anything but I'd rather just go home, even if Ron would call me crazy. My parents should be worried sick by now."

They're not your parents.

The rest of my thoughts were frozen on my tongue. "Who said that?"

I felt Milord stiffen. "Who said what?"

"I thought… No. It's nothing." I resettled myself in the cushions. "I must have been hearing things." The coverlet has slipped so I pulled it back up.

The air felt tense. I felt sure he'd press the issue; force me into telling the truth about the Voice. The silence was so heavy, even with the crackling of the fire in the background.

We sat for who knew how long before he spoke again. "I wish I could let you go home but I cannot."

I was distracted from tracing those blasted paisleys. "What?" I'm sure my lack of attention was obvious in my tone.

"I would send you home if I was able to do so, but I do not have the power to grant your request. That's not how things work here. Mantaset brings those it will, and does not let them leave until their purpose is fulfilled. There is a lot about this place that even I do not yet understand."

"But you're the Master! You know everything!" I was a bit surprised at my outburst but didn't take it back. "You had me brought here. You said so yourself!"

He sighed. I could imagine him shaking his head. "No, Kas. I may have said that but it was not exactly what I meant. Even I was brought here, though for me the reason is more clear. I had a better grasp of who I am before I came here. It helps. You have been hiding from yourself your entire life, not that you could help it."

I found myself wishing I could see what this strange man looked like. For some odd reason, I wondered if he was cute. What facial expression was he using? And then I shook my head at the idea. I felt shocked that I even thought about it and let the revulsion go up my spine. I had to remind myself that I shouldn't be thinking such thoughts.

"You should let someone tend to your wounds or they might become infected," he pointed out, changing the subject.

"Someone did look at them," I muttered but couldn't hold the lie. "Okay, so maybe only at my ankle," I grumped. "That… quack! I can't remember ever being so angry in my life. Did you know he tried to give me brandy for pain? Can you believe the nerve? Talk about gross!" I shuddered at the memory.

"I wouldn't worry about him if I were you. He has departed the premise. You might say he was 'kicked out'. Though I admit it was rather entertaining to see how you reacted to him." Did I detect a hint of laughter in his tenor voice?

"You were watching the entire time?" I leaned forward as I spoke in disbelief. Part of me was saying, "I knew it!" The other part was simply outraged at the lack of privacy.

"Not in the way you are likely thinking. I happen to have a way of knowing things without being where they are happening. It complicates things at times, but it does make it easier to supervise those under my care."

I rubbed one hand down my cheek and shook my head. "I don't get you, I really don't." Why did I feel comfortable talking to this strange ghost? It was weird. Something must be wrong with me.

My feelings confused me. What was going on here? Forbid if I was actually starting to like him. After all, I was supposed to hate him, wasn't I? I mean, come on! He kidnapped me, right? Or was I suffering from Stockholm Syndrome? Wasn't that what it was called? I couldn't remember.

"I think you should return to your room. You look tired," he advised. I wasn't sure if this was for my benefit or for his, though.

I had to admit I did feel tired, despite my supposed nap. I wasn't sure if it was because I'd over exercised my indignation or from some other reason. My eyes were starting to droop anyway, despite my attempts to stop them. Or had they been doing that the entire time? "I'm not tired," I denied.

"Shall I summon someone to carry you, or would you prefer to stumble down the hallway on your own?" I caught a hint of definite amusement in his voice. Was he laughing at my strong will? Would he call me stubborn? Chances were good he would.

I mumbled something that not even I was sure meant anything intelligible. The drowsiness was creeping into my being like some kind of spell. Was he a magician? I was content to just sink into the cushions and stay there, if he'd let me. I closed my eyes. After some time, I don't know how long, I felt myself swaying in someone's arms as I was carried back to my room.

CHAPTER EIGHT

THE FOLLOWING MORNING DAWNED BRIGHT and clear, despite the glittering snow-covered grounds. I ate a breakfast of what I hoped was egg-battered toast and apple juice. My appetite had returned from the previous day. I think it had to do with the fact that my ankle didn't hurt as much. Jenny had made an herbal poultice for the pain that seemed to numb more than just nerves.

Jenny had learned I was set in my determination to be independent. She left a set of clothes on the bed instead of trying to help me dress. They consisted of a pair of squarts, a skirt-like pair of ankle-length pants, and a whitish blouse. My newly acquired boots lay next to the wardrobe. The cane was right next to them.

I wondered at the choice of apparel, but, not wanting to hurt her feelings, I put them on. They made me feel a bit more like me. I had always liked the half-and-half approach to style. Dresses were for Sundays and special occasions like weddings, not every day wear. I hoped this meant they'd have pants too.

The sound of someone knocking on the door broke my silent reverie. When Jenny answered it, a man whom I'd never seen before stood in the doorway. He was about six feet tall. His face was clean-shaven and tanned. I wondered what he could want with me and expected him to apologize for knocking on the wrong door.

"You are Kas?" he inquired. He obviously had not knocked on the wrong door. "I am Huntsford, Master of the Horse. I have been sent to escort you on a tour of the stables."

"Um, okay," I replied, puzzled, wrinkling up my face as I spoke. "What do I have to do with stables or masters of horses?"

Huntsford cleared his throat. "My Lord required it of me to see that you receive some fresh air by way of a tour of the stables. His mind is his own and I need not try to explain his reasoning. It is enough for me to hear and obey his will."

Great, brainwashing. Was this my eventual fate too? And what was with the over formal way he spoke? Talk about weird. But a change in location would be nice.

"Sure, why not?" What did I have to lose? I picked up my cane. "How long of a walk is it? I need to know whether to find a stiffer pair of boots or not. These ones seem to be softening a bit more than I'd like," I noted without looking at him.

"It is a fair pace, but there is no need for you to walk. I will carry you." He didn't give me time to protest. Instead, he draped a long cloak over my shoulders and picked me up like I weighed nothing, carrying me down the hallways and stairs. His stride was long and we covered the distance quickly.

One of the footmen opened the main door for us but did not follow outside. When we passed the area where I knew there should be some thorn bushes, I felt my scabs throb but didn't say anything. I did a double take when I realized the bushes weren't there. And, from all appearances, they never had been there to begin with. My skin prickled even more when I realized where Huntsford was taking me, down a tunnel of high arching stone.

"Not much farther," Huntsford said in my ear. I was just glad he wasn't wearing a hood. That, and the fact that the archway didn't have cracks all through it, saved me from jumping out of his arms and trying to run away for all I was worth.

We entered a small clearing where grass covered all but a three-foot wide area of beaten earth. I didn't like the looks of it anymore than I had the tunnel. But at the far end of that section sat a set of high doors that looked nothing like what had been in my dream. One door was open and I could smell dry hay coming from that direction. Among other things. I wrinkled my nose.

Huntsford pushed the door open even wider with a booted foot, making sure I didn't hit into the frame. "Welcome to the stables, Milady." My eyes popped out, almost literally.

The stables were immense, just like everything else in this place. Hundreds of horses were stabled in separate stalls; each stall looked large enough to hold two horses or more. A long walkway went down the middle. It was wide enough to allow several horses to ride abreast of each other. There was also still enough room for the benches that were placed every fifty or so feet.

The Master of the Horse left me on one of these benches, and then walked down the long walkway, disappearing around a corner. I huddled into my cloak and wondered where the exercise part for me came in. So far I'd been carried. He hadn't allowed me to walk a single step. Huntsford had gotten far more exercise than I had.

I was snapped back from my thoughts by the sound of a horse snorting. I looked up to see the most gorgeous horse I'd ever laid eyes on. She was pure white, except for the almost silver star on her forehead, and her mane and tale, which also looked silver. Man I loved that color, always had.

Beauty was a queen's animal, or a princess's at the least. Her long silky mane reached down to her flanks in silver cascades. I wouldn't have surprised to see a pearly white horn sitting between her ears. But there wasn't one.

She nickered, and then stuck her warm nose into my lap, letting me feel her shiny coat. "You're so beautiful," I whispered into her mane.

"She is, is she not?" Huntsford walked around from what seemed to be behind her, a smile in his eyes. It was hard to tell. The horse was so big.

"I've never seen anything like her." Granted, I'd not had much to do with horses. The only exception was the neighbor's mare. I looked up with longing at her smooth features, noticing she was already saddled. "I wish I could just look at her forever."

"Would you not rather ride her?" He looked at me with a funny little quirk to his eye. "That is the only true way to learn about her."

There was no way he wanted me to ride her. That was insane! "Oh, no. No. I couldn't." I shook my head for emphasis. "She's meant for someone far greater than I ever will be. No, it's better not to even think about it."

"Milady, she is your horse. She will allow no other to ride her," he coaxed. "She was meant for you."

"No. No, no, no, no." I shook my head in alarm. "No way!"

"She was yours from the moment she was foaled. Do not deny her what she has so longed to have."

"No, you don't understand." I rose to my feet, pressing against the bench so I wouldn't fall over. "I've never ridden a horse in my life. I don't even know how. Besides, who could teach me to ride one worth beans? It can't be done. I'm a hopeless cause, and with this ankle of mine--"

"It can be done, Milady," he countered. "The Master had already guessed at this. Your horse is the gentlest creature and will not let you fall. The Master trained her himself. Do not fear. I will teach you. It will be as though you were born in the saddle." He seemed to be in total earnest now there was a scary thought.

I looked around, hoping to find some kind of escape, realizing I was near the middle of the building. It couldn't have been an accident, purposely thwarting what I had in mind. Man, they were good. "All right! I'll let you teach me. But I'm a slow learner," I sulked.

Huntsford laughed at this and lifted me into the saddle with ease. I felt like I'd floated up there instead of being lifted. "There you are little mistress. She becomes you."

"I should think not," I retorted, but then I looked down. "Wow," I exclaimed. The horse shifted under me. It was a long way to the ground. I swallowed, realizing I had twisted my fingers in the long mane. "I feel like I'm going to fall at any moment."

"Beauty won't let you fall," he smiled as he snapped on a leader rope.

"Beauty," I breathed. The name was perfect. I couldn't have chosen any other. Unfortunately, her name did not ease my fears. My hands still twisted in the long hair. The lurch under me as Huntsford led Beauty towards the stable doors was unnerving.

"Today, I will take you on a tour of the grounds," he stated. "There are many things to see, even in winter. Tomorrow, I will begin to teach you how to ride."

"Tomorrow? You're kidding, right?" I blinked at the strange look he gave me.

"Do I look as one with four hooves or with thick, course hair?" He'd stopped walking.

"Uh...." He saw my confusion, though I can't say who was more confused, him or me. Apparently the lexicon of my own time, world, whatever, was not the common one here. "You know... joking?"

He seemed to ponder before answering. "When one says another is kidding, it is thought that he or she is speaking of his or her goat. It is the term used when a female goat is with child. It would seem that it is different from where you were raised." Yeah. Talk about understatement. I gave a nervous laugh then fell silent. "But yes, tomorrow I shall begin to teach you the art of the true equestrian."

Once again, he started out for the many different gardens. I was too surprised by what I saw for much talk. Huntsford seemed to prefer it that way anyway. All the flowers were in bloom despite the snow. Each garden seemed to specialize in one color, and there were decidedly a lot of them. They had to have somewhere in the realm of fifty different teams of gardeners to cover them all.

One garden was filled with pink flowers, another with all yellow, and so on until I'd run out of names. I was disappointed to find there wasn't a single rose bush anywhere. Roses have always been my favorite flower. Oh, that's not to say there weren't a whole slew of other flowers. There were. I noticed daffodils, iris, lilies, blue bells, and pansies, to name a few. Oddly enough, there was even a bed entirely devoted to dandelions. And everyone I knew said they were weeds.

I sighed heavily. Beauty rolled her ears back at me. It made me laugh. "You silly thing." I scratched behind her ear. She looked back with appreciation. "No roses," I murmured to her. "Not a single one." I guess they weren't welcome there, unlike all the others. Even if they had appeared in my dreams.

CHAPTER NINE

HUNTSFORD CAME FOR ME AFTER breakfast for the second day in a row. I should have guessed he'd come because of his comments from the day before. Jenny had once again lain out an outfit with a split skirt. I'm sure she realized it would be easier for me. I didn't have the confidence of sitting sidesaddle, as I'm sure ladies were supposed to. She'd also reapplied the same kind of poultice from the night before, probably noting the swelling of my ankle.

Once we reached the stables, I couldn't do much to help with the initial saddling. Or anything like that either. I did watch as Huntsford settled the leather in place, explaining the mechanics and what the various pieces of tack were for. I began to wonder if riding without reins would be less trouble, but I drank up every word spoken anyway.

I was desperate to remember everything he so patiently taught me. And his patience surprised me. He answered my stupid questions, repeating instructions when I was overwhelmed. Something told me he must have been a wonderful father. He was old enough to be mine, after all.

Perhaps he realized yesterday's ride had been hard on me because he didn't lead Beauty far this time. We only visited the closest gardens. I spent most of the day on a stool, my foot resting on a padded bench. From there, I brushed out her soft coat, over and over again. That was just fine with me. My ankle throbbed from hanging in a stirrup. Sitting on a stool, I could at least prop it up on something.

The next day, Huntsford put me back in the saddle, after I'd tried to put on the reins. It was a lot more difficult to do than I'd thought it would be. After I'd finally got the infernal thing on, he left me for a minute, just sitting in the saddle and looking around. The ground felt even farther away without him there to catch me if I fell.

I was startled to hear a soft whinny behind me and twisted see behind me. The movement almost unseated me but Beauty sidled enough to keep me in my place. Huntsford had been right about her not letting me fall. I was relieved.

Beside me, Huntsford smiled. I hadn't even realized he'd left as he urged his mount forward. He rode a chestnut stallion of about the same size as Beauty, perhaps older though. "How is your ankle," he asked after introducing his mount. The horse's name was Kora.

I looked down at my stiff booted appendage, feeling the pressure of the stirrup holding it in place. "It aches a bit," I admitted. Somehow I felt like being honest with him. I didn't even think to lie. Of course, he probably already knew.

"Let me know if your ankle pains you further and we will turn back," he replied. "It would not do to prolong its healing by overworking the appendage."

Turn back, my mind mused. Turn back from what? Where were we going? But before I could ask out loud, he reached over to help me situate the reins in my hands. My fingers shook as he placed the leather strips in them. He didn't have to say anything for me to know he really did expect me to learn how to guide my own horse. But even with that realization, my hands gripped the leather and my back went rigid.

"Try to relax," he advised. "Beauty is able to sense your tension." He was right. She was acting just as uncomfortable as I felt. He urged his mount forward and I tried to understand how but my brain didn't want to grasp the simple concept. Maybe I was thinking too hard.

"You control your horse's 'head' to show direction," he said. "Hold the reins back too much and you will injure her. Relax your grip and gently lean on either side to direct her. She will respond accordingly."

I still held my arms as stiff as boards, my face anxious. "But how do I make her move forward?" Thinking about how to control her movements completely knocked out the curiosity of where we were going.

Huntsford's blue-gray eyes were emotionless as he looked at me, but his expression softened. "You do not 'make' her do anything,' he admonished. "You may urge. You may ask. To force your mount is to ruin her." I looked down. "But to persuade her to do as you ask, that is what I will teach you. But you must trust yourself as you come to trust her."

My stance didn't relax anymore than it already had, but his words did sink home. I was committing them to memory so forcefully I didn't see him move around me again, coming up on my other side.

"Squeeze with your knees," he suggested and I looked up in surprise. "It may help to give an encouraging click with your tongue. You may also try flicking the reins. In time, the two of you will create a language that you both understand."

I decided to try his first suggestion, barely squeezing with my knees. I leaned forward, as if that would somehow convey my desire to move in that general direction. Beauty took a step and Huntsford seemed amused as he laughed at my reaction.

He clicked his tongue and Kora walked forward. "Come," he said. "Much of what I will teach you is best taught out of doors."

I tried adding the tongue clicking to my knee squeezing. It unnerved me when Beauty responded by following them outside. I'd almost forgotten about the snow, even though I wore a cloak. The wind was chill against my face but we continued to walk outside, following my teacher. I was a bit surprised and pleased that I seemed able to lead Beauty. At least this far. Perhaps I could be taught after all.

Every day after that, I found Huntsford at my door. He always came at the exact same time. And every morning I found myself waiting for him to come, to carry me until my ankle was up to walking. I had no idea how long that would be, though.

It should have surprised me how fast I seemed to learn to trust him, to trust Beauty. I only wondered why this was the case, just as I wondered why the saddle sores I developed didn't seem to hurt like they should. Those sores left as I became used to the saddle. And my ankle healed.

Everything seemed to change, but so subtly that I almost didn't realize it. It didn't take long for me to begin to wonder if my life had ever been any different than it was now. When did I stop seeing the castle as a prison? And why had it only taken such a short amount of time? Had there been something else before all this? I wasn't sure.

Weeks passed in a blur and it became hard to distinguish one day from the next. Milord didn't so much as trouble my dreams. I suppose he was somehow relieved I'd accepted this existence. I didn't hear my Voice either, but only part of me missed it. It was almost as if it was a part of me that no longer existed.

Then, there came a day when Huntsford didn't come. I fretted, causing Jenny to worry. I paced my room, feeling restless. I hadn't realized how much I'd come to depend on our daily rides. His companionship was something different from what I got from Jenny. It was like a strong breeze. He was gentle, but commanding at the same time. He was someone who deserved respect. I was more than willing to give it. In return, he gave me what I needed, a place to belong.

I waited for over an hour for Huntsford to appear as I sat at my writing desk and played with the quills there. "Why doesn't he come," I asked with impatience. I felt more desperate than impatient.

I needed the escape and the activity our outings had brought. I needed the openness of the castle grounds, to feel the cool breeze on my face. I needed it more than anything. The walls felt more closed in without that promise.

"It's the first day of spring," Jenny said, as if that explained everything. I didn't get it and she didn't offer any further explanation, but I couldn't sit idle. It would drive me crazy.

I stood, my mind made up. I would not return to the pathetic existence I'd had before. "Okay then, I'll just go without him."

My words seemed to shock her. "But! My lady, Kas! What if you were to become lost? Or your horse throws you?" Her eyes were bright with worry. I'd never noticed before, but it dawned on me that she was just as uncomfortable with the idea of riding as I had been at the first. I felt I needed to reassure her.

"I won't go far." My voice was steady, which pleased me. Riding with Huntsford was one thing. Riding alone was a completely different matter. But he had said Beauty would never let me fall and I trusted him. And I trusted Beauty, even if I didn't trust myself.

With great reluctance, Jenny agreed to my plan. It wasn't like she had much of a choice, once I'd made up my mind. I wasn't confined by the need to have someone carry me around anymore. I could come and go as I pleased. I had just become so used to riding with Huntsford that the idea of going on my own was just weird.

***

I walked the familiar hallway leading to the main doors. I was surprised when I went outside, though. The snow was completely gone. There had still been several inches on the ground only the day before. Jenny had been right. It was the first day of spring. I wondered what other surprises waited for me on my ride.

One of the stable hands hovered nearby as I saddled my horse and led her to the great doors. I'm sure there was a slight look of disapproval on his face, maybe because I was alone but I couldn't be sure. "Thank you," I told him when he didn't leave immediately. "I can manage." He turned away with abruptness, but made no comment as I put one foot in a stirrup to mount.

Once settled in the saddle, I sighed. Beauty whickered and I patted her neck, then urged her forward. We moved out of the shadows cast by the tall eaves and into the sunlight. I was surprised at the grasses that met me. They were already tall enough to tickle the bottoms of my boots. The individual blades had shot up almost during the night.

Ten minutes of steady walking brought us to the open fields where Huntsford had taught me to gallop. He had raced me across what had then been a vast expanse of white. Today, it was a field of wild flowers and light green grass. In the far distance hung the fringes of the forest. It was a place Huntsford had never taken me. When I'd asked about it, he'd never told me why, just that it was a place we did not go.

Beauty became restless as we just stood there. She dug at the ground with one hoof. My words to Jenny rang in my ears. I won't go far. How far away were the woods? No matter how far we'd ridden, they'd never seemed to get any closer. Maybe that was only because Huntsford had never aimed for them. I wanted to find out.

I hesitated, the reins hanging in my hands. Beauty turned her head back to look at me, nodding over and over, as if she were trying to get my attention. Her quiet whinny was impatient. "All right," I said with a smile. I clicked to her and urged her forward, asking her to canter. With a thrilled response, she shot forward, nose pointed to the horizon. I only had to hold on and wait to reach my destination.

It didn't take long. Definitely not as long as I thought it should. Before I knew it, we were facing a wall of dark, leafy trees. The trees were not all the spruce and dark pine I'd thought we'd see, but ancient trees of a different variety. Their leafy branches expanded out into giant umbrellas over the shorter furs. I guess they were hemlock and sycamore but I wasn't sure. Trees weren't my thing. And only a few yards away, sat a break in the seeming impenetrable wall of foliage. If it weren't for the tall grasses, I'd have thought it was the beginning of a path.

I dismounted, sliding down Beauty's flank. Huntsford wasn't there to keep me from falling so I had to be extra careful. I held the reins as I walked, leading my horse towards the break. Holding my breath, with heart in my mouth, I wondered what I'd find on the other side of the trees. We stepped past the first branches, through knee length grass, and entered an almost perfect oval meadow.

Wild flowers swayed in a slight breeze I almost couldn't feel. The breeze scattered through the grasses. Somewhere, in the background, I could hear the low rush of water. Birds chirped as we walked further in. I dropped the reins. I almost felt at home, in a way I hadn't ever felt before. I felt like I belonged here. Somehow, this place wasn't part of the rest of the convergence. I wasn't sure how I knew this, but I felt it was true.

I ran forward and knelt in the middle of the clearing, near a small strand of violets. I brought one of the long-stemmed flowers to my nose to drink in the wonderful scent. Beauty nibbled at the tall grass, content to stay near me. She nuzzled the ends of my hair.

I spent more time there than I'd intended. It was so easy to forget myself and everything else. To just stare up into the perfectly blue sky and feel the blades of grass gently tickle my skin. After a while, my stomach reminded me about trivial things, like lunch. I didn't want to go, but my body's complaint won over because I hadn't brought anything to appease it. But I promised myself I'd return, no matter what else might happen between.

Jenny looked disapproving when I finally got back to the castle. She served me a somewhat cold lunch. Maybe she was trying to reprimand me, even if she didn't say anything. It was easy to imagine her disapproval. Even though I'd come to value her and her companionship, I wouldn't allow it to keep me from further exploring my discovery.

Huntsford was still absent the next morning, though I didn't let that bother me. I found I was almost glad he wasn't there because I knew he wouldn't come near the forest. And, every day, for a week, I returned to the meadow. Only I thought of it as my meadow.

Late one afternoon, I gathered together a handpicked bouquet of wild flowers. The grasses brushed against my ankles as I walked towards the opening in the trees. It had become as much a comforting thing for me as anything growing up had been. I wasn't paying attention to what was in front of me. My feet knew the path without me having to look. But this time around, there was something there, blocking the path.

I stopped short, a shadow meeting me halfway through the break. The flowers slipped from my limp fingers, landing on top of each other like pick-up sticks. It was strange to think of such an image, like it belonged to a fairy tale or some other story. I couldn't take my eyes off of the path ahead of me, or, rather, the strange man who stood there.

This man was tall, five or so inches taller than me, and slender but well built. He had the kind of shoulders a girl could cry on. His light reddish hair moved in the breeze in an almost mesmerizing way. But it was his eyes that held my attention. They were deep eyes, green and perfect, with little flecks of dark amber. I could drown in those eyes.

He wore a tunic-like shirt over dark breeches, also green. He had a cap on his head with an emerald-green feather sticking out from the side, like a hatpin. It reminded me of the painting I'd seen back at the castle, the Robin Hood one I noticed my first night there. The eyes were similar, but more alive.

The stranger looked just as surprised as I felt, staring with uncertainty in my direction. Then he swept a low but graceful bow, sweeping off his cap as he did so. The long feather stirred the grasses but didn't fall out. The next moment, he was by my side, gathering my fallen flowers and handing them to me. An almost shy smile touched his lips. I took the flowers without thinking, unable to break my gaze from his face.

"Please, pardon my intrusion," he said with a voice that ran like bells, tenor bells. "I did not expect anyone to be here." I think he was about my age, or maybe a few years older. I couldn't be sure.

I blinked a few times. I tried to remember how to breathe again as I turned to put the flowers between the loops of the reins, hoping they wouldn't fall again. Part of me didn't know if I cared. He'd help me pick them up again, I was sure.

It registered in my mind that it was possible he'd known about this place long before I had. A sense of sadness washed over me, knowing the one place where I'd felt like I belonged wasn't really my own. I grabbed onto the edge of the saddle and closed my eyes. I turned my face toward the hardened leather and tried to will the sudden pain away. I felt unsteady on my feet.

"Are you all right?" He placed a hesitant hand on my elbow. It was clear he didn't understand. How could he? "Are you... unwell?" I could feel that he was uncomfortable, or was it concerned? I couldn't tell for sure. His hand was gentle and warm on my skin.

"I'm fine," I said and opened my eyes with a sigh, relaxing my grip on the saddle but not trusting myself enough to let go yet. My voice lashed out faster than I'd intended, even though it was nothing compared to the tone I might have used a month ago.

He removed his hand, even if it was slowly. I could tell I'd hurt him somehow and wouldn't help but feel sorry. I took a deep breath and let go of the saddle, leaning against Beauty's flank as I turned, eyes downcast. "Forgive me," I said. "I didn't mean to be sharp. You just surprised me and I'm not used to having others around much."

I looked up into his eyes, pleading, hoping he'd understand. I was struck again by the depth of his eyes, drowning in them. I gasped like a fish out of water. He blinked and I was released. I noticed his expression was confused, perhaps troubled. "Do you often come here," he asked, his expression not changing. I figured he was trying to make small talk, to fill in the awkward silence.

I wasn't sure how to answer, but my lips spoke before I could think. 'Only this past week. I didn't know anyone else came here." I offered this last bit as token apology, especially if this was his special place. It certainly had become mine.

He waved a hand. "Every now and again, I have come," he said in response. "It has been a while. I seldom find time." I wasn't sure what to make of that answer, but at least it didn't rule out the idea that the meadow was free for the taking.

I looked to the sky, noting the sun's position. "I should go. Jenny will worry." I made to mount but he moved closer to help me, cupping his hand for my foot. He lifted me into the saddle with ease. I felt tall in the saddle as he looked up at me.

"Will you come tomorrow?" he asked, still staring up at me. I wasn't sure if he was hoping I would or wouldn't. It was hard to read his expression.

I decided to answer truthfully. "I don't know."

Huntsford might return in the morning and I knew he wouldn't ride near this place. I wasn't sure which alternative I liked more. While I'd formed a bond with Huntsford, it was more the father-daughter kind than anything else.

And then there was this green stranger. Just thinking about him made my heart want to pound, though I wasn't sure why. But I knew that if I could, I wanted to see him again.

CHAPTER TEN

I FELT IMPATIENT AS I paced my room. The firelight crackled and danced with the long shadows. Jenny had made no comment when I'd returned late for lunch. It wasn't her place to rebuke me, though I thought I'd seen a hint of disapproval on her face as she'd brought my decidedly cold dinner.

But now I paced. I could almost see his face if I tried. His piercing eyes were the clearest part, deep and impenetrable. I'd tried to compare his image with the painting in the hall, but no matter how hard I tried, I couldn't find it. Perhaps that's why I felt so ill at ease.

I wrapped my arms around my chest, pulling the dressing gown around me. Who was he? Part of me wondered if I'd dreamed him up, if I'd just dozed off in the meadow and dreamed the whole thing. I had nothing to assure myself that he was real. I settled on the edge of my bed and contemplated my feet, wiggling my toes. I didn't even remember if he'd been wearing shoes or if he had gone barefoot. I wondered if he had hairy toes.

Jenny came in, ready to blow out the lamps and candles. "I was wondering if there might be anything you would want before I turn in," she said. I noticed she seemed a bit more intent in expression than usual, her eyes scrutinizing my face.

I tried to compose myself as I answered. "No, thanks." I wondered if I'd be able to sleep.

She looked at me for a moment but finally turned away. "As you wish. Good night, Kas." She closed the door behind her, glancing one last time at my face before leaving. I wondered what she saw but didn't dwell on it.

The morning came late. I'd tossed and turned most of the night. A sense of despair welled up every time I let my mind tell me that the man from the meadow couldn't be real. And with that uncertainty filling my heart, I found myself pacing my room far earlier than usual.

But even though the night was long, the morning light finally filtered in through the windows as I stared out them. The light had not yet touched the grass that lay several stories below. It was likely only five or six in the morning. And though I enjoyed bathing myself, in tepid water no less, I felt restless.

My long hair was dry before Jenny came knocking on the door, bringing with her my breakfast, a thin porridge and milk. It almost felt like she thought I was sick or something. She set the tray on the writing desk, as usual. I crossed over from the window to eat. But I had little appetite and played more with the spoon than I ate.

Jenny tended to the fire while I fussed with the milk cup. She glanced up every now and again, trying to keep her face neutral. Somehow, she'd changed since I'd first met her, taking on the qualities of a diplomat. I saw her purse her lips out of the corner of my eye and knew she was biting her tongue.

"Go ahead, Jenny," I sighed. "You might as well say it." I knew she'd keep it bottle up inside until she either burst or something else happened. Either way, it wouldn't be pretty.

She looked up, a child caught with her hand in the cookie jar. I smiled as I contemplated the wardrobe. I wondered why I hadn't noticed the difference in her attitude before. But she surprised me with what she chose to say next.

She stood from poking the fire and turned to face me. I guess she thought it better that way. Who knows? "You will ride again this morning?" Her voice was just as guarded as her action.

I sighed, letting out my breath, realizing she wasn't going to speak her mind. Perhaps she held too much of her former self to take such a leap ahead. "I don't know," I answered.

Don't go.

The Voice was faint but unmistakable. Why had it been silent all this time?

He does not exist. It will only be a disappointment to you when he doesn't come.

A small part of me despaired at those words, words that confirmed my fears. But another part of me rebelled against that logic. There was only one way to find out for sure. I would have to go and see for myself.

I made myself wait until after lunch. I did my best to stay occupied and ignore the almost silent whisperings that this was all a pointless venture. I paced the library, reading odd verses from a poet I didn't know. Finally, I gave in and changed into the riding skirt.

After an even longer than usual canter on Beauty's back, I sat in the meadow, my back turned towards the opening through the trees. I feared disappointment and didn't dare look.

Beauty grazed on the long grasses, the soft sound of her whickers created the only noise out of place. There wasn't any wind. I had braided close to a thousand strands of grass together, or so it seemed. My fingers mangled my last creation, my mind wandering, slowly drifting away as I dozed off.

My eyes flew open and my back went rigid. At first I wasn't sure why, but there was a prickle of something at the base of my neck, like I was being watched. I turned to look behind me but only saw Beauty nuzzling the grass several yards away. She hadn't appeared to move, and I saw nothing else that could have caused that awful sensation.

I let my breath out in relief. It was probably just my imagination overworking itself. But my breath caught in the middle of my exhale as I realized what had startled me in the first place. It was the sound of someone breathing. Someone who wasn't me. Someone who had been standing or kneeling behind me but who wasn't there now. I could feel the heat of someone's presence still lingered there.

I listened, straining for any sound I knew shouldn't be there. But there weren't any. "If someone is there, you'd better come out," I warned but nothing happened, except that I felt unnerved. I fancied a pair of eyes staring out at me from the trees. Dark eyes.

After a few moments, I stood, a bit unsure on my feet from sitting cross-legged too long. The pins and needle sensation of my lost circulation returning wasn't unpleasant. But I knew it would make my steps uncertain for a while. If something was out there, I wouldn't be able to run.

I looked over my shoulder as I went to get Beauty and wrapped my arms around my chest, vainly hoping for the impossible. The air felt chilly to me, causing goose bumps to run down my spine.

I gathered Beauty's reins, feeling disappointed and drained as I leaned against her side. He hadn't come. Why hadn't he come?

I felt too leaden to mount and I was tempted to just lean against her the entire way back to the castle, if I hadn't felt edgy. Apparently Beauty felt a bit edgy too. She sidled a bit but never far enough that I couldn't lean against her warm flank.

We headed for the break in the wood. My steps were heavy and made Beauty nervous; at least that's what I tried to tell myself. I didn't want to add fuel to my imagination's already roaring fire. I tried to convince myself that there was no reason for my heart to pound and my ears to strain for the smallest sound. Even my tensed muscled had to be caused by some trick.

Something rustled in the trees and I froze. My fingers caught in Beauty's mane and my knees locked. My heart pounded loud enough that it soon became impossible to hear anything else. I thought about wolves, like the ones that had chased me through the forest so long ago. I saw the grasses moving, ever so slightly, near the break. They swayed, but not from any wind I could feel.

A figure entered the clearing, someone wearing a dark cloak with a deep hood that looked far too familiar. My breath stuck in my throat. Images of flaming eyes filled my mind, a semi-circle of shrouded men bending over me, their faces hidden except for one.

Everything went dark and I was swimming under miles of black water, unable to find the surface. And yet, despite this, I felt calm. Something in the back of my mind whispered that the cloak had been the wrong color. It hadn't been black, or even dark brown, but a deep forest green. But a faint hint of laughter tinted my calm a harsher shade.

I resurfaced from the void, gasping like a fish out of water. At least that's what I felt like I was doing. Someone was chaffing my wrists and I sat up far too fast as I opened my eyes. It left me feeling light headed. "Ugh," I said, putting my hands to my temples.

"Are you all right?" The light tenor voice sounded of bells in my head, a voice I'd never thought I'd hear again but, impossibly, was. "Perhaps you should lay back down for a little while."

I looked up into his beautiful green eyes. "What happened?" I felt disoriented as I tried to stand instead. He held out a sturdy hand to help me, realizing I had no intention of following his advice. I ended up leaning against him for support.

"Careful," he said in my ear. "You fainted. I tried to reach you in time, but must admit I was not quick enough." I thought I heard a hint of chagrin in his tone. "I am not sure if you hit your head or not. I could not tell through the grasses. Thankfully, your horse had sense enough to remain still."

I pulled away from him with some reluctance, to assess myself. I shook my head to see if anything rattled. Everything appeared in working order. I was still a little unsure on my feet but nothing hurt. "I guess I locked my knees," I admitted. "But I'm okay now."

I turned, surprised to see Beauty standing next to another horse, one that was a rich, dark brown. The color reminded me of fudge brownies. I didn't think horses were usually so friendly with each other, unless they knew each other, but I could have been wrong. It seemed as if they were already friends. I was sure this gentleman, whatever his name was, hadn't had a horse with him yesterday so their behavior was totally at odds with what my brain said should be going on at that moment.

Realizing that I still didn't know who he was, I turned back to face him. "Um, thank you… whoever you are. Who are you?"

He looked surprised as I asked, though I wasn't sure why. He seemed to cock his head to one side. It was as if he were listening to someone I couldn't see or hear. "I beg your pardon," he finally apologized. "I hadn't realized I never formally introduced myself. Please allow me to do so now." He swept another one of those elegant bows as he continued. "My name is Christoph Letori Reilar."

I dropped into a curtsy to match his bow without even thinking about it. "Kas Lee Stanship," I said as rose, more sure of myself now. "Pleased to meet you." He smiled and I smiled shyly back.

"Your dinner will be waiting," he reminded.

I looked up and realized the sun had disappeared from view. It was now somewhere behind the trees. The slightest hint of peach tinged the sky. "Wow," I exclaimed. "I didn't realize how late it was." I turned back to Beauty and sighed as I reached for the bridle. My fingers felt a bit numb as I grabbed them.

"Allow me," Christoph said. He lifted me up into the saddle before I could so much as protest. The wind kicked up, cold against my skin and I shivered. He unfastened his cloak and handed it to me. "Here. Please take it. I would not want you to catch a chill."

I took the garment and pulled it over my shoulders, dropping the reins to do so. He handed the fallen strips of leather to me once the cloak was situated. "I do not know if this will affect your decisions," he hesitated, "but I will not be here on the morrow. My own lands need my attention. It is not something I feel I can delay."

I looked down at my hands. Even more strongly, I felt a sense of connection to him, one that I definitely didn't understand. Somehow, it was as if my heart and soul belonged to him. This was silly, of course. I barely knew this man. But hearing he wouldn't be there in the morning made my eyes prick as if with tears.

I felt his hand on my knee and looked down to note the calluses on his fingers. "Are you sure you are all right?" His eyes held my gaze the moment I looked back up. His concern was more than evident. His eyes searched mine. I had no idea what he saw, if he saw anything beyond the reflection of himself there.

"You should go," he said. "It will be dark soon." He looked away, towards the trees. It was almost as if he was searching for something. I tried to follow his gaze. Realizing that neither Beauty nor I had moved, he turned back to us. "Kas, you must go. Night is a time to be indoors." There was a sort of odd note in Christoph's words. It was a pleading and a warning.

I nudged Beauty with my heel and we broke free from the trees at a walk. He followed behind after mounting his own horse. I hesitated at the outskirts but, without a word of explanation to me, Christoph leaned over and put his hands on Beauty's crop. He said three words to her that I couldn't hear, and then stepped back. Almost immediately, Beauty launched into a gallop, taking me home. I looked back as we bounced away, but he'd already disappeared from view.

CHAPTER ELEVEN

I COULDN'T SLEEP AT ALL that night. Rather, I only slept in short spurts that were more dozing than sleep. I hated it when I did that. I could never feel like I'd rested when that happened. But even though I only dozed, I still dreamed. And I dreamed about Christoph.

We stood opposite each other. A wide ravine or chasm spanned between us. He was shouting something at me, but I couldn't hear what. A fierce, howling wind was blowing. His expression showed frustration as he tried over and over to convey his message, but the windswept his words away every time.

The wind was coming from behind me, pushing me ever closer to the edge, despite my efforts to stay put. Part of me wanted to get closer, to catch what Christoph was saying. Whatever it was, it had to be important or he wouldn't look so earnest. I leaned further out and saw his eyes widen in fear. He pointed towards me but I didn't know what he was trying to say.

And then it didn't matter. I felt someone coming up behind me and I turned around. But as I turned, I took a step too close to the edge. I tried to backpedal but the ground crumbled underneath my feet.

Before my eyes could register who was there, I was falling. I thought I saw, for the briefest of moments, someone in a dark hood peering over the crumbling edge, just staring down as I fell.

—✻—

I woke before I hit the ground, my heart pounding. It had been a long time since I'd last dreamed about falling. Dreaming about it now came as a shock. It took a while to bring my pulse back down to normal. When I could finally focus on more than just breathing, I noticed Jenny asleep in a chair next to my bed. I was glad I hadn't screamed. The sound would have woken her.

Part of me wondered why she was there. She had her own room, which was next to mine. She usually just stayed there during the night. Was it possible she'd had a bad dream too? I didn't think she was that much older than I, though I could have been wrong about that. With those thoughts running in my head, I was able to fall back to sleep.

—✻—

It was raining in a steady stream by the time morning came around. The landscape was streaked and hard to see through the window. Even if Christoph had not said he wouldn't be in the meadow, I wouldn't have gone out in that downpour.

Instead, I went to the library to find a book to read. I took a long time looking, listening to the rain beat against the windowpanes. Despite the sound, it was too quiet.

Even with the grandfather clock ticking in the hall. I took the book back to my room and spent the morning reading it. If anyone had asked, though, I wouldn't have been able to tell him or her what it was about.

Jenny brought me some strange grog that night. "This will help you sleep,' she told me. "I have noticed you have had trouble doing so these past few nights."

I took the plain cup, some kind of stoneware. It was hand fashioned. I could feel the lines of the finger grooves from whoever had made it. The liquid inside was dark and murky looking. It smelled strange but Jenny waited for me to drink it so I took a sip.

And almost spit it out. I made myself swallow the mouthful I had, my eyes watering. I had to gag to make it go down my throat. It tasted awful! It was something I'd imagine Ron to drink, a combination of dirty socks, rocks and pickle juice. How could my sister ever have even considered marrying him?

I didn't finish the drink, nor did I need to. My eyelids were already heavy from the herbs she'd used. Jenny had to grab the cup before it fell from my limp fingers. Whatever that stuff was, it was potent. My eyes slid closed and the next thing I knew, it was morning.

The rain continued, much as it had the day before. I felt myself going stir crazy from the confinement. Trying to ease my boredom, I decided to explore the castle more fully. I already knew how to get to the library, and to the main entrance, but that was where my knowledge ended. Something would have to be done about that.

After finishing a breakfast of porridge and toast, I set off to explore. The rain made it oppressive and I had to ask Jenny to find a small lamp for me to carry. Part of me wished for a flashlight, or even electric lights. Part of me was perfectly fine with the handheld oil lamp. Had I really split into two different people? And if so, where was the other half?

Knowing I had a whole day ahead of me, I took my time to examine every piece of artwork, every suit of armor. Secretly, I was hoping to find that Robin Hood portrait again. Unfortunately, I wasn't able to find it, no matter how hard I looked. And believe me, I did. With a full day to kill, I probably explored at least a good chunk of the castle. But, not really knowing just how big this place was, I couldn't be sure exactly how much I'd really seen.

I did find it strange that most of the doors I came across were locked or barred by something on the other side. Hadn't many of them been open earlier? Back when I'd first come here? Or was that all part of a dream? Or, had I somehow managed to find a completely different part of the castle? I wasn't sure. Either way, all that walking wore me out and I decided to go to bed early.

The same dream returned that night. At least that's what I thought at first. I saw Christoph across the gulf, shouting something at me. Again, I couldn't hear what he was saying. And, like before, I sensed something behind me. When I turned around, I caught a glimpse of a horse. The beast pawed the ground, his nostrils flaring as he whinnied with a high-pitched scream of rage. And on his back....

I couldn't look but couldn't pull away either. I felt ash in my throat as I looked at him. White-hot ash. His eyes were filled with dangerous silver and copper flames. And he was laughing. He widened his eyes and I could see a dark pit of immeasurable depth inside them. He blew fire at me, like someone blowing out cigarette smoke. Scorching hot metallic fire. There was only one way to escape. I stepped back into space.

The air rushed past me. It moved so fast that my lungs couldn't grasp it. My body screamed for air. I flipped over and saw the ground rushing up to meet me. I threw my hands out to ward off death and found myself sitting up in bed, sweat pouring off my body. My heart was pounding. I could see dark red flames dancing out of the corner of my eye.

It took me a moment to realize Jenny was by my side, washing the sweat from my face with a cold cloth. I shivered and the flames were gone. "It was only a dream." Her soft voice slowed my beating heart. Her touch was so gentle but couldn't stop my body from shaking.

"It was so real," I whispered, unsure of my own voice. "It was so real."

"Shh… It's over now." She crooned to me, much as I might have crooned into Beauty's ear if she'd been startled by something.

I fell back against the pillows and closed my eyes. "Why is it so cold?"

Jenny didn't answer. Instead, she pulled the covers around me. "You should try to sleep." I felt her words instead of hearing them. Even with that, I wasn't sure if she'd spoken at all. I don't know why but I sensed a change. Jenny was not the same as she was even a week ago. Or my perception of her was not the same. It reminded me of my mother, but not quite. The caring for me in distress was the same, but the feeling was not. I felt at home, but I knew this was not my home. I opened my eyes.

"It's all right to sleep," Jenny coaxed. "I will ward off any more night terrors. Trust me." She handed me a cup like the one with the grog she'd made the other night.

Without thinking, I took it and sipped the liquid inside. It wasn't quite the same as before, but held a similar flavor. I felt my vision streaking in front of me, like the rain was washing my consciousness away. When I opened my eyes again, it was morning.

———

The rain had stopped and the clouds appeared to be breaking up, but it was still damp out. I hadn't been out in over two days and was definitely going stir crazy. I had to get out, even if it was only for a little bit. At least that's what I told myself.

I announced my intentions to Jenny, who was less than pleased. But she gave in. Maybe it was because she saw how desperate I was to be out of doors. Or, maybe it was something else. I wasn't sure and I didn't care. I just wanted some space, away from the oppressive castle and its darkened halls.

———

By the time I'd gotten ready, it had begun to drizzle again. I wore a woolen riding skirt and overcloak, but nothing to cover my head. There was a hood but I didn't feel like wearing it. Instead, I let the water just stream down my face. Despite Jenny's grog from the night before, I was still tired. I didn't care.

Beauty and I bee-lined it for the meadow, even though I'd promised not to go far. I was hoping to see Christoph again. I waited for several hours in the rain, but he didn't come. I felt abandoned, forsaken.

My heart wanted to break and my mind wanted to beret me for my wishful thinking. Why should he have come back? Part of me thought it was weird that I wanted him to be there. I barely knew the man after all.

Then I remembered that the last time I'd seen him, he hadn't come until later in the afternoon. That thought gave me some hope. I wanted someone to hold me, comfort me, and tell me everything would be all right. Jenny wouldn't do. Neither would Milord, if I could find him. I needed a man, someone I could see with my own eyes and not just hear or feel.

I settled down to wait some more. I watched Beauty forage for a while and then take a nap under the trees. I envied the ease of her life. I bet she didn't have strange dreams about falling off of cliffs or madmen with flaming eyes.

———

After a while, I realized my legs had fallen asleep and I had to thump them back to life. A light rain began as I paced the meadow until I was soaked, even down to my petticoats but I didn't care. I would wait until he came, even if it meant I had to stay into the night. It was highly irrational of me, I know, but it felt right.

I lost track of time. The rain did not let up, keeping the sky clouded over. Despite the cold, I found I was getting tired. I usually wasn't able to sleep when it was chilly but I couldn't keep my eyes open any longer. I slept.

———

The rain stopped. It must have been late. Beauty had left the meadow. I figured she'd made her way home to hot mash and a warm stall. I could walk back alone.

Picking up the edges of my skirts, I waded through the tall grass, heading towards the path through the woods. I didn't like the look of the trees, even though they weren't overly thick. I almost thought I heard someone following me but didn't see anyone.

I moved away from the trees, across the castle grounds. I hadn't realized how vast they were. I wouldn't reach the castle before full dark but I would try. Someone would come looking for me before too long, I was sure. And if not, it would only be a matter of time before I returned.

I trudged along through the dim light of evening. My existence became lifting one foot in front of the other. I was so involved in this simple act that at first I didn't see them as they followed behind me. But after several minutes, I could hear them. I looked back.

Their hooded faces stared after my progress. It was clear they wanted to catch up to me. Their pace quickened and so did mine. I still remembered the hideousness of the faces. Or should I say lack of real faces? It didn't matter. They had stared at me with such hate that night I dreamed of the horseman of fire that it still gave me chills.

I ran, stumbling over my waterlogged skirts. They kept pace, gliding after me in their dark robes as if floating, instead of running.

The castle seemed so far away. I would never it make it. Their harsh laughter seemed to confirm my assessment. They would reach me first.

I tripped over something in my path that I couldn't see. Almost instantly they were surrounding me, laughing. It was if they'd been waiting for this to happen. Dark fear ran through my veins and I could not move.

The leader came over to me. He knelt by my side and lifted my chin with a gloved hand. "You are mine," he said. I almost thought I recognized the voice but I'd never heard anything so evil before now.

"I am my own," I returned, trying to sound brave. "You don't own me."

He lifted me to my feet by forcing my head upwards, hand still holding my chin. "You are young and naive. You are in a world that is not your own. I can do what I will. Own what I want. I claim you."

"But I don't claim you," I retorted, trying to summon up any anger I could. I remembered my fiery indignation when I'd first met the Master, Milord. I pulled on that bitter feeling, holding to it like a stinging nettle you can't let go of. "No one may claim me but me. I claim myself. You can't make me do anything I don't want to do."

He snarled. "You will fear me and obey. You are mine!" His men moved in closer, tightening the circle around me.

"No I'm not! You have no power over me!" My fingernails dug into the palms of my hands as I clenched my fists. I think they broke the skin.

"Deny me and I will destroy you," he warned.

I moved away from his hand and glared into the shadow of his hood. "I may not know who I am but this much I do know. I am not yours and I will have nothing to do with you."

He let out a roar of rage, a sound that went beyond physical sound. I covered my ears, cowering to try and keep out the awful sound. It vibrated through my bones, ran in my veins, shattered my thoughts into useless shards.

The circle of men completely enclosed me, their robes billowing out towards me with a chill wind. I felt a cold hand circle my heart and squeeze. Ice filled my lungs and I couldn't breathe. I stared upward with glazed eyes, gasping like a fish out of water. Their eyes glittered in the shadows. I would have screamed if I'd had breath to.

Lightning flashed through the sky, thunder slicing through the silence. The light dazzled my eyes and I couldn't see. I felt myself falling again. Falling… Falling… a frozen mass of nothing.

"Kas. Kas. Come back to me, my love."

I swam through thick shadows, searching for the light I felt touching my skin. I gasped as air filled my lungs. I coughed. Water ran down my face and I shivered. I struggled to open my eyes.

It was full dark, the stars hidden behind the still crying clouds. I saw trees surrounding me, blurred but discernible.

Many people moved about the meadow. My meadow. I couldn't see their faces but I saw their outlines in the torchlight. Two people leaned over me. One was chaffing my wrists. The other was crying over m. I think she was praying.

"Jenny," I croaked. My throat felt raw. I felt like I couldn't get enough air. I tried to move. My body ached and I groaned.

"Milady," Jenny breathed. "Kas." And she burst into fresh tears. "We thought you were dead."

"No. Not yet," I tried to joke. "Just cold." I coughed again.

The other leaned closer, a torch lighting his face. "Huntsford."

He nodded. "We must remove you to the castle. Are you able to sit on your own?"

I tried, my body creaking. Sweat broke out, even with the drizzle. I raised myself a few inches but fell back. I was dizzy and burst into more coughing. I tasted something metallic on my tongue.

Huntsford and Jenny exchanged worried glances. "She must be moved," he emphasized. He motioned for several men to come over and help. One brought over Huntsford's horse, which he mounted. He signaled to the men to lift me into his arms.

Several others also mounted horses. I saw Jenny mount Beauty with reluctance. I wondered how Beauty had gotten here. They wouldn't have brought her back would they? Had she left at all? I'd thought Jenny didn't know how to ride.

I felt Kora heave under me as I was settled into place. Huntsford's arms were on either side of me. One of his hands held me in place while the other held the reins. Other horsemen escorted us back to the castle. I don't remember arriving.

CHAPTER TWELVE

MORNING LIGHT SHOWN DOWN THROUGH the high windows of my room. The curtains were open. The sky was clear. I felt as though I'd endured several nights of horrible dreams. They were dreams I could barely remember, like wisps of smoke that are, and then are not.

I rose from my bed and pulled on the light robe left for me. A cup of hot cocoa waited by the fire, with a bowl of sweetened cereal. I sipped the warm drink, musing to myself.

I felt like I'd been throttled in my sleep, but other than that, I felt fine. The day was warm and I couldn't resist the call of my meadow. Jenny didn't want me to go, but the day was warm and I would not be kept indoors. Dreams, or reality, from my short-term memory had faded into unreality. She tried to talk me out of going but made sure I had a good lunch packed before riding off. I was too stubborn for persuasion.

Dew covered the ground but, other than that, it was not wet. The rain had to have been a dream, or I'd slept several nights on end. I didn't know which reality to believe so I let them be.

I directed Beauty into a brisk trot and let her just roam. Time was ours to spend. The grounds were immense. We didn't reach the meadow until early afternoon because we explored. But we weren't alone when we got there. Christoph was there.

I saw him bending over his own horse, loosening the girth and sending him to forage in the tall grass. I dismounted and walked into the clearing. Beauty nickered and he looked up.

His green eyes held mine. I felt my heart beating and realized that breathing became harder. I wondered if he felt the same way. He blinked and time restarted. He bowed and I inclined my head. It felt cheesy but, at the same time, glorious and appropriate.

"What are you doing here?" I asked. I gave him a mock suspicious face, one brow quirked in inquiry.

He returned my look with one of earnest disapproval. "I might ask the same question of you. I was told you would be staying indoors today."

If I hadn't been so off kilter by that statement I might have noticed how wonderful his voice was, light but strong. When had I started to see him in that light? Had I always seen him that way? Strong but soft? Warm and gentle?

"Oh really," I replied. "Who told you that?"

Christoph raised his eyebrows in innocence. "The maids, footmen, ladies in waiting, cook, scullery maids… any one of them might have told me."

I let Beauty loose to forage. "Are you spying on me?" I wasn't entirely upset with this idea.

He seemed surprised. "Spying? I may have inquired

from time to time, but I have never spied. The servants sometimes offer more information than they should." He seemed amused by that for some reason.

"Do you live in the castle?" I started to circle him like I'd seen cops do in movies. "And do you enjoy following me around, including in my dreams?"

"So it is to be an interrogation," he smiled. Christoph was definitely amused. "Would you prefer I sit or stand?"

I stopped in front of him. "I don't care. I just want answers."

He smiled. "As you wish." He settled down onto the grass, as if he didn't have a care in the world. He had to look up because I refused to join him. "No, I do not live in the castle. This is not my home. You might say I'm… visiting."

I detected a hint of irony in his voice. "And your answer to the second question?"

"Who is following whom? The day we first met in this meadow was as unexpected for me as it was for you. And today I had thought you would not be coming."

I played with the tall grass, running the blades through my fingers. "But you knew I come here often."

He smiled. "I will not deny it."

I wandered a few steps away, flustered. I couldn't put my thoughts together. I whirled around, cheeks flaming. "And who are you? How do you play into all this?"

Christoph's expression changed from playful to more serious. "There are some things you are still not ready to hear."

Still? What did he know? He was a stranger. He talked like we'd discussed this before. It wasn't possible. We'd only run into each other a couple of times. The wheels in my head were turning, probably too quickly. My hands clenched and unclenched.

"Kas," he called out. "Don't."

I strode up to him, glaring. "Who are you really? And why do you act like you know me so well?"

His expression was pained. "I cannot tell you."

I put my hands on my hips. "Can't or won't?"

He won't.

The words echoed from multiple points. Why was there more than one voice this time?

"Why don't you leave me alone!?" I yelled as I spun in frustration.

Christoph flinched away, as though I'd hit him. Except I hadn't meant to include him in my tirade and it hurt that he thought I had.

He won't. He won't. He won't, the Voices chanted.

I closed my eyes and saw the hooded men bending over me. They were laughing. I opened my eyes.

"No," I said in a whisper. "No. This isn't real. It isn't right. No!"

This couldn't be happening. Not again. I turned and ran towards the castle, forgetting that Beauty was there and would be much faster.

"Kas, wait!" Christoph might have reached out a hand but I didn't see it. I just wanted to get away from the Voices. It was a shame. He thought I was running away from him. But the truth was I didn't even know why I was running. I just had to get away.

***

I ran down the path, not paying attention to where I was going. My eyes were blinded with the tears I'd wanted from the beginning. Traitor tears. I ran into something blocking the end that opened up onto the grounds. It was something dark, something supple. My fingers met rough cloth.

"Kas." I looked up and saw the leader of the hooded men. He reached out a hand, his fingers closing into a fist. Was he wearing a metal glove?

I couldn't move. I couldn't breathe. I couldn't do anything. There was no sun, no sky. The trees were gone, the dirt and rocks. Everything. There was nothing else, just him and me. We stood in a black, soundless void.

"I hope you have reconsidered my offer. I allowed you to live to give you a second chance," the hooded man said.

I heard voices whispering in my mind. They were indistinct and faint but the occasional phrase came through.

"Hold on, Kas. Hold on. Don't leave me."

"I won't," I wanted to say, but couldn't. All I could do was stare into those horrible eyes.

He waited.

You didn't spare me, I thought. You didn't want me to live. Someone else kept you at bay. I realized the truthfulness of this as I thought it. Someone had kept this monster at bay. And part of me knew whom.

He acted like he had not heard my thoughts, which was just as well. "I give you until the morrow to make your final decision. But first, a reminder of what I can do."

Pain ripped through my body. I wanted to cry out, arch my back, anything to find relief. But I couldn't. I was completely at his mercy.

Then, suddenly, I could arch my back. I could breathe and I could scream. I closed my eyes against the pain and screamed, electric fire coursing through my veins.

I heard footsteps around me, rustling cloth. My eyelids were heavy and would not open. I didn't know if I wanted them to. What if he was still there?

"Don't worry, my child. He is gone. You have nothing to fear." It was a feminine voice again. The one I'd heard in that one dream before that quack doctor came.

I felt someone's arms around me, holding me. I clung to the feeling, despite my fire tingled skin. I felt so helpless. Tears ran down my cheeks and were wiped away by a gentle hand.

"*Shh… Don't cry. They're only dreams.*" The voice was not Jenny's. Whose was it?

"*They won't harm you. Shh… Not while I'm here.*" Her sweet words lulled me to sleep.

Morning came. I did not see it because the curtains were closed, but I felt it. I opened my eyes and struggled to sit up. I felt like I'd been lying in bed for ages.

It took a moment for my body to obey. But was I awake? I was aware of the possibility that this had all been one long dream and nothing more. But did I want to wake if that was the case? Could I?

Jenny was asleep. She lay slumped over in a chair that someone had pulled up to my bed. She looked exhausted, her usually tidy hair dangling down her face. Several guttering candles and lamps lay scattered about the room. I sensed some kind of battle had been fought here. I wished I knew who'd won but there was no real way to tell.

I left my bed, trying to be as quiet as possible, but it was hard. The slight exertion winded me. I felt like my entire body was creaking with disuse as I walked the few feet to the nearest window. And my limbs were shaking long before I reached it.

I pulled open the curtain with effort and was almost blinded by the light pouring in. I had to shut my eyes against the glare. The warm sunlight felt good against my skin.

Half remembered dreams floated before my closed eyes. I opened them to shut out the visions, shaking my head to clear them away. I didn't want to remember.

I leaned against the window and tapped the glass with my fingers. It was too quiet.

Without disturbing Jenny, I found some clean clothes in the wardrobe and changed. My hair was in hopeless tangles. I just wanted to yank it out with impatience but made myself take the time to brush out all the snarls. I could have used a bath.

The hallways were empty. My bare feet didn't even make a sound as I went to the library. No one crossed my path. The air felt heavy, like everyone was asleep or waiting, even the castle. What if Milord was sleeping too? What if he wasn't home?

It took a lot of effort to push open the library doors. I was panting before I had them fully open and had to take a moment to lean against the hard wood so my lungs could catch up with the rest of me. My head hurt.

Taking a deep breath, I entered the library, walking to the great fireplace in the first room. The roaring flames were the only source of light and sound, even though they seemed smaller than before. The high windows were shrouded against the morning sun.

I walked to the hearth and traced the edge of the mantel with my fingers. Why was it so quiet?

The walls faded into light mist and I heard sounds, a baby crying.

"Sh… little one. Mother has you. You're safe."

As the mist cleared, I saw a woman with long, dark hair, like mine, holding an infant in her arms. She was rocking the child and humming a song I'd never heard before but somehow knew. She began to sing. Her sweet voice brought tears to my eyes, though I couldn't explain why.

"Hush, sweet child, no harm will fall. Safe in my arms, sleep once more. Fear not nightly sound, nor strange face. When you wake, gone

I'll be, but still there, guiding your feet."

As the melody ended, the woman gave the child to an older woman. It seemed to me that she was reluctant to part with the baby.

The other woman cradled the infant and tried to comfort the mother. "My lady, I will make sure no harm befalls your child. She will be safe until it is time."

The mother nodded and stroked the baby's cheek, then turned away. She sobbed. "Oh my child! My sweet Kas!"

I opened my eyes and felt as though I'd just broken through water. I didn't know if I could trust my ears.

"Kas."

I turned around too fast. The room spun and my knees melted like jello. I sort of slid to the floor but bent to press my head against the ground. I squeezed my eyes closed, willing my stomach to settle.

I heard Milord walk over to me with rapid feet. I felt his hands touch me, support me.

"Forgive me," he apologized. "I did not mean to startle you but you should not be here." He helped me to my feet and walked me over to one of the couches. I leaned against him, still bent over like a limp rag doll. Why did my body feel so heavy?

"What's wrong with me?" I panted as he settled me into the cushions. I felt him sit next to me, the cushions tilting as he sat. He stroked my hand with invisible fingers. It was a bit disconcerting, but only a bit. I liked his gentle touch.

"You caught a fever. It would not surprise me if it had been caused by your ride in the rain. It may have been from something else. On that point, I am not sure. But you were weak, vulnerable. I had no idea he had grown so strong." This last bit he said almost to himself. I wondered whom he was talking about but an image flashed before my eyes. I shuddered.

I felt him lean forward and clasp my hand. "What do you see?"

How did he know I'd seen something?

"A man." The words slipped off my tongue without permission. "His name is Kishan." I didn't know the name, I was certain. But I knew I'd heard it before. I blinked and the image was gone.

"What do you know of Kishan?" Milord's voice was intent, almost watchful. I could hear it in his tone.

I tried to think. "He's… He's a hooded man who steals souls." Somewhere deep inside, I knew there was more to this but didn't dare look beyond what I'd said.

"Yes," Milord confirmed. "But some might say he destroys them. He is a dark wizard with many talents, none of them good. It is unfortunate that you have caught his attention."

I felt a lump form in my throat and I almost couldn't speak. "But why would he want to destroy me?"

Milord was silent for a moment, and then he squeezed my hand. "Because, you, of all people, pose the greatest threat to him."

"But why?" Why would such a creature feel threatened by someone who didn't even know who she was? It didn't make sense.

Milord sighed. "Because of who you are."

"But who am I!" I cried out in frustration.

"Oh, Kas." His voice was heavy with emotion. "I wish I could tell you, but I cannot. And before too long I will have to send you back to your home, but not yet. You are not strong enough yet."

I looked up. "You mean I get to see my family again?" The thought brought a small ray of light into my fear-darkened mind.

"As you know them, yes. But first, we must make you strong again. We almost lost you last night, Jenny and I."

We almost lost. The battle. It was between dark and light and He had almost lost, lost me. I felt dizzy again.

"He held you within his grasp for so long, I was afraid it was too late. His barbs run deep. I had never seen them so deep before. He has been reaching for you for a long time."

I swallowed the lump in my throat. "How long?" How long had I been suffering like this? I had to know.

"It has been three weeks," he answered. I almost wished that I could see his expression but was glad I couldn't.

I let out a groan of anguish. Had all those dreams been true, then? Or products of a fevered mind? Or were they Kishan's 'barbs' to torture me? Had Christoph been a dream too?

"I do not mean to frighten you. His presence still lingers, but he does not have the same hold over you that he did before. You are strong; otherwise you would have been his long ago."

"He said I was his," I whispered, remembering that confrontation in the fields outside the castle. I shuddered at the thought.

"You belong to whoever you choose," Milord answered. He probably heard the unasked questions in my thoughts. Was I really that strong? And did I really have a choice?

CHAPTER THIRTEEN

MY MIND BUZZED FOR THE rest of the day. I'd learned so much in such a short span of time. And even though Milord had said Kishan no longer had as strong a hold on me, I knew the battle wasn't over. If I really did present that much of a risk to him, he would try again, and with more firepower behind him. I didn't like that idea.

Even though I had just been ill, unconscious for weeks on end, I decided to go out. It was against all advice, especially Jenny's. I didn't bother asking Milord's thoughts on the matter. I'm sure he would have told me no and done something to bar me in my room. I wasn't going to have that, so I didn't tell anyone.

Huntsford was tending to a foal when I entered the stables. He looked rather surprised to see me there but gave a bow anyway. "I see you have recovered," he said as I moved to collect Beauty's tack and saddle. "It is good to see you on your feet again."

I smiled, feeling a bit self-conscious. Part of me wished he'd been my real dad. "I never got to thank you for bringing me back," I hesitated as I moved to Beauty's stall. "I know you don't like the forest."

Huntsford inclined his head. "Though it is true I do not like those trees, when it is in the service of someone in my care, I will not hesitate." He stood and brushed off his hands, the foal settled next to its mother. "I see that you will ride out again. Would you like me to keep you company?"

I shook my head. "No, thanks. I have a lot on my mind and need to figure it out all out. Maybe another time?"

Huntsford smiled, realizing I wasn't trying to snub him. He walked over and took my hand, kissing it. "My Lady, I would ride with you any time you desire."

I smiled with happiness. If nothing else, I definitely didn't want to lose his friendship. But he wasn't the one I wanted to talk to about my recent discoveries. Nor was Jenny. I needed someone who was closer to my age, someone likely to be more practical in these manners. I needed Christoph. If he was real.

With a farewell wave, I set off towards the vast fields. Huntsford had made sure I'd packed a saddlebag with water and food. How he knew to have them ready, I'll never know. He was just like that. Prepared.

After meandering for about an hour, to make sure no one was watching, I turned Beauty towards the forest glen. I let her gallop, enjoying the sensation of my hair flying out behind me. Who cared that it wasn't washed? I could take care of that when I got back. It was nice to feel free and unconfined.

As I'd hoped, I saw Christoph's horse, Delphi, as soon as we entered the meadow. But I didn't see Christoph. Looking around in confusion, I finally dismounted and walked the edges of the meadow. I'd never ventured under the trees. Something told me it wouldn't be a good idea.

The grass swayed behind me. I could hear a shushing noise as I turned. Not sure who or what was making the sound, I was tempted to run, though I wasn't sure how far I'd get.

I gasped in relief as I realized it was only Christoph. "Would you stop doing that!?" I protested.

Christoph was all but laughing as he walked towards me and put his hands around my waist. Before I could protest, he'd lifted me into the air and twirled me around several times. "I thought I might see you here today," he confessed as he set me back on the ground.

I had to put one hand to my forehead as the dizziness his actions had caused subsided. Apparently I wasn't as recovered as I'd felt. "I hoped you'd be here," I replied, a bit out of breath. I was just glad he wasn't a dream. I don't know if I could have endured that disappointment.

He took one of my hands and led me towards the far end of the meadow. "Come. I sense you have something to tell me." He released my hand as we reached a large blanket he'd spread out over the grass.

I sank down onto the soft cloth, glad for the chance to sit. "How is it you seem to know more about me than you should?" I asked, only half expecting an answer. Chances were good that he'd just divert again.

Christoph almost flopped down beside me, his tall brown boots smacking together at the heels. "Sometimes you as easy to read as an open book," he informed me. "And sometimes you are as mysterious as poetry from the masters. All that aside, what have you on your mind, milady?" He took off his cap and swept an awkward bow. I couldn't help but idly realize just how awkward it was to bow from that angle.

I had to laugh. Was it the little things like this that made me like him so much? Was it that he was so gentle and kind? I wasn't sure. His skin was so fair, and yet I knew he was a hard worker. I also knew that there was more to him than met the eye.

Christoph leaned closer, catching my gaze with his mesmerizing eyes. "What troubles you? I can see it in your eyes that something does."

I quickly looked away so I wouldn't drown in his gaze. Instead, I played with my skirt, wadding it between my fingers as I told him everything Milord and I had discussed that morning. I went even further to explain what had happened since I'd first come to Mantaset and the Waymeet of Worlds. He listened attentively, as if he were drinking in every detail and contemplating everything with equal attention.

It took a long time to explain everything, but he didn't interrupt. If it had been Jenny, she'd have interrupted at least half a dozen times. It was just her way.

It was nice to not worry about that, to just get out everything that was in my heart. I left out the parts where we'd been together. I'm sure he didn't need to hear my perspective on them. Besides, I'd only feel embarrassed.

Christoph nodded at all the right parts. I could tell he was listening. He seemed most interested in my accounts about Kishan and his hoard of hooded horsemen, as well as the Voice I'd heard all my life. "I wonder," he commented, twirling a strand of grass between one thumb and finger. "Is it possible that your Voice and this Kishan are related?"

I had to blink in thought as the idea filled my mind. Was it possible that they were connected? Were the voices even remotely similar? When Kishan had confronted me in person, he'd sounded so downright evil. My Voice had never sounded that way. But it had some definite similar qualities.

Sitting back, Christoph used his elbows as supports. "It is a possibility, is it not? I am not saying it is so, mind you." He raised his brows at me. "But it is most definitely a possibility. And it would explain so much, would it not?"

My hands were still as I contemplated the possibility, my skirt still wadded between my fingers. Milord had said Kishan had been reaching for me for a long time. Did he know something I didn't? I had to chide myself over that thought. Of course he knew more than he was saying. He'd pretty much admitted to it. The question was why.

"Was I gone for three weeks? I mean, that's what Milord told me, that I was sick for three weeks," I hazarded. "Is it true?"

Christoph cocked his head to one side, as if he were listening to something. "Time is relative, is it not? What to one seems such a long time may not be so to another. If you recall, you did mention that when you first arrived, time did seem rather a mess. Does it matter how much time has passed?"

"It does to me," I wanted to say, but didn't. Sometimes he could be just as infuriating as Milord was. "I just remember Kishan telling me he would come for me on the morrow. But if three weeks have passed since then, has he already come, or is he still waiting?" Thinking about that made my head hurt.

Christoph sat up and looked at me as if he were contemplating something. "It is possible that he was kept at bay, unable to come at you. Undoubtedly, he will try again."

My heart sank as my opinion was reflected in those words. "I still don't understand why, though," I complained.

He gently took my hand in his, massaging the back of it. "Think about it this way, you pose some kind of threat to him. It may be he fears you or what you may become. Or, he feels that you will keep him from achieving some goal he is trying to attain."

I pulled my hand back in frustration. "But I have no idea what any of those reasons could be! Just how in the world can I threaten him! I mean, I'm just Kas! I'm just Kas." I felt tears prick at the corners of my eyes.

Christoph took my hand back into his own. "But is that all you are? You have been told that you are stronger than you believe to be true. You have been told that there is more than you see, to which I agree. In the end, I feel that it is not a matter of if you know who you are or not, but if you believe what both Milord and I have told you. There is more to you than you are aware. Much more. And when you are ready--"

I rolled my eyes. "When I'm ready. I'm getting sick and tired of that, you know. It's a broken record. 'When you're ready. When you're ready,'" I mimicked. "And when will that be?"

He set my hand back down. "I do not know," he confessed. "You are approaching a great crossroads in your life. Only you can decide what direction you take."

I pondered those words as I rode Beauty back to the castle. I wasn't sure I was any closer to understanding than I had been before. And that was frustrating. But at least I wasn't alone in this. Before I'd left the meadow, Christoph had kissed me on the forehead, promising to do what he could to help me. I wasn't sure how much of a promise that was, but it helped.

I spent the next few days indoors. After arriving back at the castle, I'd discovered I definitely was not as recovered as I'd thought I was. To make up for it, I confined myself to my room. Jenny and a book were my constant companions. No one else bothered us, which was just fine with me.

Jenny was a bit surprised by this, but didn't question it. She attended to me without any changes from the usual. She talked when I wanted to talk. She was silent when I wanted silence.

After the third day, I began to feel stir crazy again. Jenny could see it, but I was sure she still wanted to keep a close eye on me. Remembering my theory that she wasn't a fan of horses, I invited her to ride out with me, just to see what she'd do. I even tempted her with the notion of meeting Christoph, who I'd finally told her about.

Jenny had declined, just as I thought she would. But, after several more days of badgering her about it, she finally agreed to at least come and watch. I was elated, like I'd scored some kind of victory.

Unbeknownst to her, I'd been conspiring with Huntsford to get her back in the saddle. The fact that she'd ridden Beauty when they'd found me too sick to move in the meadow told me something. She already knew at least the basics. Now I wanted to know just how much she really knew.

Huntsford was waiting for us in the stables. He'd already saddled his Kora, leaving Beauty for me to prepare. While Jenny was watching me cinch the buckles, he brought out another, smaller horse that was also already saddled.

"No! No! No!" she protested when Huntsford but the reins into her hands. "I cannot! I cannot!"

Laughing in amusement, I mounted Beauty and made her circle both Jenny and the mare Huntsford had brought from another stall. "Oh come on, Jenny," I coaxed. "I know you know how to ride. Indulge me?"

Jenny's eyes had gone wide but she couldn't refuse Huntsford's help into the saddle. She sat on the leather padding, looking just as uncomfortable as I had felt the first time I'd ridden Beauty while Huntsford mounted Kora.

I moved closer to her, letting our horses sidle next to each other. "I promise we'll be nice," I offered as an apology. It had been a while since we'd ridden through the gardens and I'd made a special request that we do so.

Hearing the plan, Jenny was more agreeable. I think she was relieved we weren't headed towards the meadow.

We took things slow. I wasn't sure how much Jenny knew about riding and didn't want to press my luck. Chances were she was already mad at me for this little joke anyway. I didn't want to push it too far.

———

Once again, we rode through the various gardens. There was a wider variety this time around. Maybe it was because of the different season. I wasn't sure. But no matter how hard I looked, I still couldn't find a single rose bush. Part of me was relieved. Kishan couldn't pull them out on me again. Unless those bushes hadn't been here at Mantaset. But how could he have taken me elsewhere?

I discussed this issue with Christoph later that afternoon. Jenny had been a bit worn out from the ride and was more than happy to let me go and do my own thing. Once lunch had been finished, I'd headed back to the stables.

Christoph hadn't brought the blanket today. Instead, he leaned against a large stone and played with the wild flowers. "It is a most intriguing notion," he admitted after I'd addressed my concerns. "What do you think happened?"

I pulled back to keep from leaning too close to him. I was sitting beside him, also idly playing with the flowers. I held one with the stem between my fingers. "I don't know. I guess it's possible," I allowed. "I mean, Milord did say that this was a convergence, where all realities collide."

Christoph smiled. "Go on," he encouraged.

I put a finger to my chin as I thought about it. "And if that is true about various realities, why can't different places occupy the same space too? That might explain why sometimes it takes longer to get here than on other days, or why the hallways sometimes change in the castle."

Nodding, Christoph pulled a flower close to his nose so he could smell it. "Yes. That is a possibility. It might also explain why there are sometimes servants and other people inside who are not usually there, would it not?"

I contemplated the idea. "That's true. But if this is all just a patchwork of different places, maybe this meadow isn't part of Mantaset at all. Maybe it's a random place that somehow got attached."

Christoph raised his eyebrows. "I suppose it is possible," he agreed. "Anything is possible in such a place. And if Kishan did indeed take you to another connected location, it means that somewhere such a place does exist."

I shuddered at the notion. That entire place had reeked of death. I definitely didn't want to end up back there.

"I wouldn't let such a thing happen," he assured, reading my thoughts, or maybe the expression on my face. "That kind of place is not fit for a lady such as yourself. Nor would I wish it upon you or any other."

I had to look down, a hint of warmth creeping up my cheeks. "I really wish Jenny would come with me one of these times, and meet you," I confessed.

Christoph looked towards the sky, his lips twisting in amusement. "Perhaps she does not wish to present competition."

I raised a brow at that. "Competition? For what?"

He reached over for my hand and kissed it. "Why for my heart, of course." His eyes sparkled as he spoke. It took my breath away.

"You're being silly," I admonished him. "We're just friends." We were, weren't we? That's all it was, right? I mean, what else was there?

He looked at me wryly. "Are we?"

I felt flustered at the intensity of his gaze. My heartbeat increased in both speed and intensity. It was hard to focus on anything but the sound of his voice and the feel of his fingers caressing the back of my hand.

An image came to mind. I was sitting on a velvet couch

in the library, near the great fireplace. Milord had moved to my side, something I hadn't expected. His gentle fingers probed the scabs down my arm, his voice soothing my nerves at the same time.

I shook my head to clear the image. When I looked down, I realized Christoph was still playing with my fingers and, somehow, I didn't mind. But why had thoughts of Milord cropped up? Feeling suddenly self-conscious, I withdrew my hand and sat on it. "Maybe," I answered, trying to not turn redder.

Christoph shook his head in amusement. "I see. Even so, I am sure Jenny would not wish to spoil the potential of there being something more."

I felt the tips of my hair turn beet red, or at least that's what I told myself. Was it possible to feel this warm, even without a fever? "I need some fresh air," I announced as I shot to my feet. It was a ridiculous notion, since were already outside, but I was having a hard time breathing.

Christoph didn't so much as move from his spot as I paced around the meadow. I had to cool down. Why was my heart beating so erratically? And why did the idea that he might have feelings for me please me so much?

After several minutes had passed, I finally returned to his side. He seemed just as calm and unflustered as he had the moment I'd entered the meadow that day. Why could he remain so calm when my own heart was doing flip-flops? It wasn't fair.

I pointedly sat back down, clearing my throat. "Back to the original topic, if you don't mind," I said while smoothing my skirt.

Still clearly amused, Christoph nodded. "Yes, it is possible that you entered a piece of another world in that dream. As your invisible companion said, things have an interesting way of occurring in this place. What is dream becomes reality. What is reality becomes dream. I am sure you have discovered this for yourself."

I nodded, less than pleased with the answer. "Alright

then, how about a guess why Milord is always disappearing. And why I can't see him."

Christoph seemed to contemplate that question more than any of the others. He twirled a flower stem between his fingers, first one way, and then the other. "Perhaps it is because he is not fully inside the convergence," he finally offered.

I pursed my lips, resisting the urge to just bit the lower one. "What do you mean? Is that even possible? I thought once you were here, you were completely here. I mean it's not like you leave any part of you behind, right?" How could that even be possible, I wondered.

For a moment, I thought he was going to choke on something. But he didn't. He cleared his throat with a shake of his head. I wasn't sure why that had happened, but decided to forget about it. After all, sometimes I breathed my spit at awkward moments too. And that's what it was; at least that's all I hoped it was.

I was surprised when he started laughing. "Kas, sometimes you say the most amusing things. And yet, it must be admitted that there is the possibility. Take our previous topic for an example. Is it not possible for a person, any person, to not fully be in this convergence? If other worlds are able to only partially be here, why not a man? Or a woman?"

I wrinkled my nose. "When you put it that way, how can I argue?"

He smiled with understanding in his eyes. "Though I have not been here long, there are some things that I have learned. The first is that nothing is as it seems. The second is that logic has no hold in this place."

"And the third?" I asked, rising to the bait.

The corners of his lips turned up even more. "The third is that your stubbornness will never surprise me."

I resisted the urge to slug him in the shoulder. It was something I would have done to my brother, David. And just remembering that, I felt a small bout of homesickness.

Out of all my siblings, David was the one I missed the most out of all of my siblings.

"Kas?" Christoph leaned towards me with a quizzical look on his face. "Are you all right?"

I shook my head, more to come back to reality than for any other reason. "Sorry. I was just thinking about something." I looked at the sky, noticing the sun was starting to move from view. "I should get going." I stood and headed towards Beauty.

Christoph followed me, brushing grass from his flowing trousers. "I did not mean to offend you," he apologized.

I stopped cinching up the girth on Beauty's saddle and leaned against her flank. "It's not that," I sighed. "I'm just getting tired." How could I tell him that what I really wanted right now was something I couldn't have? Sure I could talk to him like I could to David, but there was something different about it. David was my brother. Christoph wasn't.

"I am sorry," he repeated, though whether for my benefit or his was anyone's guess.

I turned to face him, not expecting him to be quite that close. He was only inches from me. I could feel the heat coming off his body. My heart beat more heavily, my breathing becoming shallower. When had he moved?

His eyes looked more intense than usual. Without so much as a warning, he leaned in and kissed me. On the lips. I stood like a deer in headlights, with no idea what I should do, my arms hanging down at my sides. His lips were warm against mine. They almost tasted like cinnamon. But I was too surprised to do anything except stand there.

After who knew how long, he broke away. "Forgive me," he almost whispered as he stepped back. "I should not have--"

I cut him off by moving forward and pressing my lips against his. I wasn't sure why I did it. Somehow, it felt like the natural thing to do. I felt lightheaded when I finally broke away.

"You should go," Christoph said, his voice choked with some kind of emotion that I couldn't attend to. He seemed flustered when I looked into his eyes and nodded, unable to speak. He had to help me into the saddle. I doubt I could have managed on my own. My legs had become rubbery.

Once again, he whispered something into Beauty's ears. After giving her a pat on her flank, my horse shot forward. I was glad I had the reins tightly in my hands or I really might have fallen off.

CHAPTER FOURTEEN

I KEPT ZONING OUT THAT night. Jenny commented several times on this as she embroidered a cushion. Finally, she put down the needle and thread and came over to feel my forehead. "You don't appear to have a fever," she commented.

I gave her half a smile. How could I tell her the real reason for my absent-mindedness? It could not, would not happen. Besides, how could I express the emotions I'd felt when his lips first pressed against mine? Or how I'd almost subconsciously followed up by kissing him back? It would not happen. Just thinking about it made me turn red all over again and that wasn't a good thing. It would make Jenny think I had a fever when I didn't.

"Perhaps it would be wise to retire early," Jenny suggested when I didn't comment. "It would be unwise to tempt fate."

Tempt fate. Hah. Fate had been tempted. Very much so. And I liked it. A lot more than I probably should have. And that was stupid. I just couldn't figure out why. I mean, it wasn't like I kissed him first or anything.

What was wrong with me? I almost hit my head on the writing desk, trying to knock some sense back into my brain. How could this have happened? Weren't we just friends? But now he'd kissed me and I'd kissed him. My world was completely shaken.

The following morning, I was summoned to meet with Milord in the library.

Butterflies filled my stomach as I walked down the empty hallway. The request had been for me to come alone. Jenny had protested, but the footman had insisted. I tried to calm my queasy stomach as I walked, but it didn't work.

The grandfather clock ticked loudly as I entered the library. I was suddenly reminded of the first time I'd visited the place. It was not a comforting memory. I'd been alone and scared out of my mind. I now knew I had nothing to fear, but that didn't keep the butterflies at bay.

Something had changed since I'd last visited Milord. I'd kissed someone. And I'd liked it.

A footman led me towards the second room in the library. I hadn't so much as set foot in there since finding that empty book in the middle of the maze of shelves. I wasn't sure if I wanted a repeat experience. If it hadn't all been a dream that was. I didn't even notice when he left.

I thought I was alone at first. Then I felt someone's presence, knowing almost immediately that it was Milord. But when I looked around, I still couldn't see anything, until I focused on the floor. It was hard to distinguish, but I thought I saw his shadow standing next to one of the bookcases near the doorway.

"Good Morning, Kas." His words confirmed my suspicions. Why couldn't I see anything more than his shadow? It was annoying, especially when his blended in with those around it.

"Milord." I curtsied to the shadows. "You wanted to see me?"

"Yes. I have something for you. Come with me." His shadow moved forward and I followed. He led me to the center of the room where the wooden table lay.

The book I'd found earlier in the year, back when I'd broken my ankle, was still there on the table. It lay in the exact same place that I'd left it in. No one seemed to have so much as touched it.

He must have picked it up because it floated over to me. I hesitated to touch it, remembering what had happened the last time I had. The book nudged me and I took it with reluctance. Nothing happened.

"This is a special book," he said with reverence. "It has lain waiting for some time. Waiting for you."

I looked up, wishing I could see his face and thought I saw a glimmer of flesh. "But there's nothing written in it. The pages are blank." I didn't voice my other concern. Why had I reacted like I had the first time I'd touched it? Or, rather, why had that vertigo happened at the same time?

"What happened when you first touched these pages was not the fault of the book. It was Kishan. He was trying to keep you from this."

"You're reading my thoughts," I accused, trying to sound teasing but didn't succeed.

"I was there." His words rang in my mind. But hadn't he once told me it had all been a dream? At least that's what I remembered. I could have been wrong. Nothing in this place was as it seemed.

"And the pages?" I prodded.

"They are for you. My advice is to record your thoughts and your feelings. Your history. You will need it.

There will be many whose path will cross yours. They may well try to convince you that none of this happened, that it could not have happened."

I blinked in confusion, holding the book to my chest. "Why?" What reason could he possibly have to tell me something like that?

"Because they will not understand."

"Who?" I tried to think of anyone who might try but couldn't think of anyone. Jenny wouldn't. Huntsford wouldn't. Who else was there?

"When you go back, you will know."

Something sunk in the pit of my stomach. I think it was my heart. "Go back?"

"Yes," he said. I could hear remorse, or was it regret, in his voice. "You are strong and whole again. I can keep you here no longer. Much as it may pain us both, it is almost time for you to leave. Your family needs you and you need them to help you learn who you really are."

"But why can't I do that here?" I didn't want to leave. Not now. This was my home now. And what about Christoph? Would I never see him again? Silent tears ran down my face. He brushed them away with invisible fingers.

"You've learned how to cry," he said. I sensed a hint of a sad smile.

"I don't want to leave." I wanted to say more, much more, but couldn't. The tears choked me so to the point I couldn't speak.

"Oh, Kas." Milord's voice was choked with emotion. "I do not want you to leave. But you must. I have no say in the matter. Even I must leave."

I tried to control my tears. "But you are the Master."

I felt his hand caress my cheek. "Of some other realm, but not here. Not the Waymeet. No one is master here."

"But you are!" I squeezed my eyes closed and felt my arms enfold him and his enfold me, holding me as I held tight enough to cause discomfort. Why was I so choked up about this? I had given my first kiss to Christoph, and yet here I was, acting like it had been Milord.

"Now listen to me," I heard in my ear. "What I am about to tell you is important. You must leave before the sun sets tonight. Jenny will have everything ready for you. Do not be afraid and do not look back. Your destiny lies ahead, not behind. Remember that."

I thought I felt his lips brush against my forehead and then there was nothing. I knew, without having to open my eyes or reach out, that he was gone. Not even his shadow was there when I opened my tear sodden eyelids. But why? Why had his lips felt so sweet touching my skin? And why did they remind me of Christoph?

I don't know how I returned to my room. When I got there, Jenny helped me out of my dress and presented me with a pair of pants and a purple button-up shirt. Their significance didn't want to sink in, even after I'd changed into them. They felt strange after wearing skirts for so long.

Jenny sobbed into a handkerchief but didn't say much. I felt like I was at a funeral. We spent a rather solemn time together, saying goodbye. After that, I gathered my few possessions, at least the ones I could call mine, and put them in the bag Jenny provided. It reminded me of a knapsack, with one deep pocket and several smaller ones. The bag was heavier than what my brain said it should be.

The next thing I knew, I was sitting astride Beauty, heading away from the castle. Why had I not gone to the meadow to tell Christoph I was leaving? Would he have tried to stop me? I hoped the answer was yes.

I didn't want to look back. But as I rode across the grounds, I turned to peer behind me. I thought I saw, for the briefest of moments, the outline of someone standing on one of the many balconies. He was wearing a green tunic over earth colored breeches. And on his head, he wore a green cap with a long feather.

Tears blinded me as we heading towards the forest. I don't know how long I rode but it seemed to take forever to reach the end of the grounds. This was a direction I usually never took, heading in the opposite direction of the meadow I had called my own. I felt a strange tingle run through my body as we stepped into the shadows of the tall trees.

The forest seemed to hold more shadows. They lay at our feet with a sinister restlessness. It made me feel uneasy but we traveled slowly for fear of the twisted roots and branches. I fancied I heard Milord as the grayness darkened around me. Or was it Christoph? I wasn't sure.

"Remember me, Kas."

Several hours later, the light was just enough to see my hand when I placed it in front of my face. It reminded me of that first time through the forest. Night had come and I somehow knew the wolves I'd fancied the first time coming through were here now. I heard the pad of their feet in front and behind us. How, I couldn't say, but hear them I did.

A break in some trees allowed the moonlight to shine through and one of the wolves howled. Beauty was spooked. She bolted as a second wolf howled and I clung for dear life. The pack Jenny had given me bounced on my back. The wolves followed, snapping at our heels. They were driving us.

We raced into a glen where more wolves waited. I'd never heard of their traveling in such large numbers before. There had to be at least twenty. And they were all nipping at us, closing in as they drove us on.

Beauty bucked in terror, rising to her hind legs as she kicked out. I clung to the saddle but the sweat on my fingers made me slip. I was falling. For the first time ever, Beauty had let me fall. I don't even remember what happened to her as the wolves moved in and I screamed. Something hard hit me from behind and I blacked out.

I woke to hard ground underneath me. A large stone pressed into the small of my back. I opened my eyes and sat up with some difficulty. My head hurt. My body hurt. Dried tears crusted my eyes. I looked around and impossibly saw the Sitting Rock only a few feet away. The family cabin was just behind a screen of trees. I could see the red roof through the leaves.

Groaning, I stood up and worked out some of the kinks, popping a few joints back into place. I didn't think I'd broken anything. I wondered how long I'd been gone, lying there in the dirt. It couldn't have been long. I brushed off as much of it as I could, absently picking up the backpack that had been lying next to me.

Dark clouds hung in the sky, threatening rain, but patches of blue still littered the sky. I walked back to the cabin and wondered why there wasn't any mud. I remembered mud, unless time here had passed too. But where was everyone? There should have been someone searching for me. Someone else should have been at one of the neighboring cabins but they seemed deserted. In fact, they seemed somehow older than I remembered.

Sharp pain seized my stomach and I bent over in agony. I wanted to throw up but closed my eyes instead. The world seemed to shift out from under me, then settle again. It was like an old film trying to orient itself, moving from side to side until it finds its place in the sprockets. The sensation stopped but I kept my eyes closed just in case.

I sat hunched over for several minutes until the pain subsided. I opened my eyes and saw mud. Several cars were parked in the driveway. Mud reached several inches up over the treads. The cabin stairs were slick, slimed over by the passage of many caked feet. I saw the skid marks where someone had slipped.

I walked up the steps, smelling grilled burgers. It felt like every joint in my body was groaning in protest. Someone had the portable grill out on the deck. The sizzling noise coming from under the hood told me that some kind of meat was cooking inside.

The door opened before I could reach it and my plumber uncle came out. He didn't so much as say hello as he went over to the grill with an empty plate. "These ones are about done," he called out as he lifted the lid and flipped the patties.

Mom saw me through the open doorway. "There you are, Kas. I was about to send someone to find you." She looked me up and down. "Did you slip in the mud?"

I blinked in confusion, and then looked down. Mud splattered the front of my pants and my backside felt damp, as did my hair. I was probably coated in mud from top to bottom. "Um, yeah. By the Sitting Rock," I improvised.

She frowned. "Good thing that's packed earth. How's your headache?"

"Better," I fibbed, rubbing at my forehead. I didn't know if I was lying or not. I couldn't remember how bad of a headache I'd had the last time I'd seen her. I definitely had one now, and it seemed to be getting worse the longer I stood there. Somehow, it looked like nothing had changed since I'd left. Minus that one weird moment when I'd thought I'd seen dry ground. Maybe that was part of a dream too. I had hit my head rather hard, after all.

"Well, take your shoes off so you don't track mud." She turned around again like nothing out of the ordinary had happened.

"Mom," I walked over to her, after removing my shoes, "how long was I gone?"

She turned around, a spoon in her hand. "I don't know, sweetie. Maybe half an hour? Why don't you see if there's a change of clothes in the car?"

I almost fell over, my mouth wanting to drop open, but I did my best to recover before she noticed. Half an hour? More like six or seven months, or more. I wasn't sure, but there was no way that only half an hour had passed since I'd left them. Wasn't there?

"Incoming!" My uncle charged through the door with a steaming plate full of grilled meat. He set the platter on the counter next to the condiments for hamburgers. I had to dodge to keep from being run over, the tails of his "kiss the chef" apron flying out behind him.

I decided to take Mom's advice so I put my shoes back on. I almost forgot about the pack still slung across my back, but remembered when it hit into the car's open door. For whatever reason, it was completely dry and free of mud. Not wanting to think further about it, I stuffed the thing under the back seat.

I thought I remembered putting in a change of clothes sometime before we'd headed up to the mountains. I just hoped it was still in there. I sighed in relief as my searching fingers found the plastic bag. It paid to be prepared.

I slammed the van door closed and trudged back up to the cabin, where I borrowed the bathroom to change and try to clean up. It was a process that took longer than I'd anticipated. By the time I was finished, all the cooked burgers were gone. But that was okay. I wasn't much in the mood for food.

I guess Mom realized something was off when I didn't go for the second round of burgers. It was not unusual for me to eat at least two at any given setting. But this time around, I wasn't hungry at all. A million different bees were buzzing inside my head. The end result was that I felt rather dizzy, and more than a little sick.

Mom walked over and felt my forehead before I could so much as protest. "You don't have a fever but you do feel cold. Maybe you go should lie down." Her eyes shown with concern. "You look kind of pale. Maybe it was from walking in the damp."

For a brief moment, I felt a different hand pressing against my forehead, a masculine hand. This phantom hand was more broad and had calluses in different places. I shook my head to try and dislodge the sensation. "Yeah, maybe you're right."

Even though it had been over an hour since I'd woken up at the Sitting Rock, my body still felt off, all creaky and sore. It was almost like I'd been thrown. I walked towards the back part of the cabin where several beds sat. Each one had a thick layer of plastic covering it. As I passed the wood furnace, I caught a glimpse of a ring of wolves circling a horse and rider in the fire. As one flame leapt up, the horse reared and the rider fell. I shuddered at the thought that it might be reflecting that odd dream I'd had at the Sitting Rock. It was just too weird to contemplate.

I rubbed at my face. "Gotta stop doing that," I told myself as I passed the first bed. I didn't want to be too close to where the action was. After all, some of the cousins were close by, playing a game of gin rummy.

I opted for the third bed in the row of four. The plastic cover wasn't exactly comfortable, but at least my head seemed to stop spinning as I lay down and closed my eyes. No more than a few minutes later, I was asleep.

Amid the various planets and stars that spun behind my eyelids, I could make out two distinct voices. It took me a moment to realize that they belonged to Ron and Sara.

"Do you really think she'd do that on purpose?" Sara's voice asked.

I heard Ron sigh. It was a sort of exasperated kind of sigh, like they were hashing over the same topic they'd been discussing for hours. "Those who are disturbed, even slightly, have a way of making sure their delusions are justified. You heard her back at your parents' place. Her voice told her not to come today. Despite that, we all came up. And what happens about an hour in? She suddenly comes down with something. If you ask me, something's not right in her head."

"She's not delusional or disturbed," Sara defended. "I grew up with her. If anyone knows, it would be me."

Ron wasn't convinced though. "Just because you've lived with someone doesn't mean they can't hide things from you. Now, I'm not saying she *is* disturbed. But there is definitely a chance she is resorting to unhealthy means to control and manipulate others. That is what I find disturbing. And it could mean there is some level of mental illness. Especially if what you've told me about her is true."

Mental illness? Ha. Ron was my case of mental illness. He was a mental illness. I had half a mind to tell him so but didn't want to move, not even to speak. The sound of my younger siblings and cousins playing became a droning that suggested sleep. My body didn't want to ignore that suggestion. I felt like I hadn't slept in years.

I was swimming through grape-flavored jello. Don't ask me how I knew. But I was struggling to reach the top. My arms were pushing against the gelatinous mass in what felt like a useless attempt to break free. What my eyes saw was dark and distorted. I couldn't make anything out.

"Kas. Kas, wake up."

I felt someone shaking my shoulder. I opened my eyes but didn't recognize where I was. "Jenny?" I asked, only seeing the vague outline of someone feminine standing over me.

"What?" Okay, that voice did not belong to Jenny. But if not her, than who?

I blinked the cobwebs from my eyes. Sara stood over me, one hand touching my shoulder. "Oh. It's you." I groaned as I rolled over and sat up. A cold chill ran up my spine and I shivered. "What time is it?"

Sara rolled her eyes. "Time to go. You missed dinner. And we can't leave until you get your hind end up and down to the van. You guys blocked us in, remember?"

She definitely sounded cross. They probably made her watch Russell because I'd dozed off. I noticed the little rascal had managed to scatter toys all over the room. Allisa and Dan were cleaning up after him. Ron was nowhere to be seen, not that I was overly surprised.

I dragged myself to the door and scraped off the dried mud from my shoes before putting them back on. I should have realized it was a pointless exercise as the sound of rain filled the background. They'd be muddy again in no time. I doubted the ground had even had the chance to solidify while I'd been visiting la-la land. Fun times.

Most of my aunts and uncles were still packing up. At least those who weren't staying the night in the drafty cabin. I was glad I wasn't planning on doing that. It took me a moment to realize Sara had followed me.

"Who's Jenny?" She sounded mildly curious, still cross though. Maybe she was just being the typical pain we all knew and loved. Then again, maybe not. There probably was an ulterior motive involved. This was Sara I was talking about, after all.

I didn't look up as I tied my laces. "No one. Just a friend from school," I grunted. I don't think she believed me. But how was I supposed to tell her that Jenny was someone from a series of dreams I'd had after bumping my head on the Sitting Rock? No way. Besides, those dreams were fading.

"So who's Milord?" She practically got in my face with that question. And that sucked because her breath stunk almost as bad as Ron's did. Okay, maybe that was an overstatement, but she really needed a breath mint.

I wished she'd go away. "No one. I don't know what you're talking about," I lied.

Sara looked smug as she put her hands on her hips, only giving me enough room to stand. "You were muttering about him in your sleep."

I tried to make my face as vague as possible. "Was I?" I stood with a bit of effort and went back inside.

She followed me. "Yes. You were calling for him. And some guy named Christoph. I'm pretty sure you've never mentioned that name before. Who is he?"

I wanted to push her out of my way. The space between the front door and the kitchen was tight. I had to think skinny to miss getting hit by an uncle carrying out a cooler. "I must have been dreaming." I ducked under the table to avoid another potential entanglement with an aunt carrying a box of camping supplies.

Sara didn't say anything else, but I could tell by her silence that she wasn't satisfied with my answer. I was just glad she'd dropped the subject. Sadly, chances were really good she'd bring this up with Ron. Yay. More fuel to the fire. Lucky me.

CHAPTER FIFTEEN

THE RIDE BACK DOWN THE mountain was uneventful. I was thankful for this, but felt a sense of loss as we drove away. It was the sharp pang of parting and I felt moisture beading up at the corner of my eyes. A tear leaked down my cheek. I wiped it away before anyone could notice.

We got back to my parents' house late. A lot later than I'd hoped, but then that's what you get when you plan on sneaking out of the family gathering as soon as possible. Not that those plans had worked out anyway. Why couldn't my little car be a little more gutsy? There was no way I'd trust that thing on a mountain road, hence being stuck with my younger siblings in the car. And why did they have to sing little kids songs the entire trip back to Brintley?

Ron and Sara followed us back down the mountain, having decided to stay yet another night. They could have easily gone home. It's not like they lived more than an hour's drive away, because they didn't. Convenience. That's all it was. They dispersed to their basement room, whispering to each other. I wasn't sure I wanted to know what they were so feverishly discussing. It might make me mad.

Mom ushered the younger ones into their beds. Allisa took some persuading. For whatever reason, she wanted to stay up and play with David, who was not cooperating with her whims. He'd locked himself in the laundry room where he'd camped out the past two nights.

I took advantage of the empty bathroom and had a quick shower. I felt like I needed a little scrubbing after coming in contact with all that mud. I suppose I could have used the tub up in the cabin, but there was no guarantee of hot water. And what hot water there was had been reserved for doing dishes.

As things stood, the cascading water felt funny on my skin, like I hadn't had an actual shower in forever. Don't get me wrong. It was nice. It was just weird. Well, except for the fact that it was cold. That wasn't nice.

I changed into my pajamas. They consisted of a two-piece flannel ensemble. As I brushed my teeth, I found myself missing the long nightgowns Jenny used to lay out for me. They were silk in texture, with a bit of lace.

I almost spit out my toothbrush as that thought crossed my mind. What was wrong with me? It had all only been a dream. Maybe Ron was right and I *was* delusional. Or I was just tired. Stress has a way of doing that to people, or so I'm told.

Mom sighed as she came to kiss me goodnight some time later. Even though I was almost eighteen, she still felt the need to tuck me in when I visited. "I don't like how pale you look," she commented. "I just hope you're not getting sick."

Yay. Fussy Mom alert. "I'm fine," I promised, trying to brush her attention aside. "I'm all grown up now. You don't have to look out for me." After all, wasn't that why I'd moved away for that all too precious freshman year? Yes I was a bit advanced academically when compared to my classmates, but who was counting?

She patted me on the head, smoothing my hair. "I know. But you'll always be my little girl." She planted a kiss on my forehead, closer to my hairline, and then headed towards her bedroom. She turned out the lights as she left, leaving me in the dark.

———

It was bright when I woke up. Morning light streamed through the makeshift curtains covering the rather large picture window. I still don't understand what they were thinking when they had that window installed. The only view was of the backyard, which was a total mess. I wished for decent curtains, anything to shut out the light so I could sleep longer.

Allisa and Russell came running through the room, screaming like banshees. They were probably headed downstairs to the basement. Chances were good they were either after Sara or something in the storage room. My bet was on the storage room. I covered my head with my pillow and groaned. Why couldn't they be quieter?

David came next. "Wake up, sleepy head. It's morning."

It was so hard to not throw my pillow. I wanted to throw it at him so badly! "Go away. I'm sleeping," I moaned from under the pillow, keeping a firm hold on it to keep me from temptation. That, and to make sure he didn't yank it away from me, blinding me.

Instead, David pulled my cabbage patch green sheet off of me. "Come on, sunshine. It's after nine," he intoned.

I grabbed for the sheet but missed. "Give it back!" I

demanded as I surfaced from the couch cushions. And I'd thought we'd called some kind of truce!

He laughed but handed the sheet over. I draped it over my arm, aiming a swift kick at his ankle. He responded by grabbing my head and giving me a knuckle sandwich. When I finally got away, I slugged him in the arm.

I muttered about stupid brothers all the way to the bathroom. Safely inside, I locked the door and turned on the fan. It was harder to hear anyone outside with that thing on.

Welcome back, Kas. I told you not to go the mountains. Was I wrong?

"I don't know what you're talking about," I answered as I turned on the faucet in the sink. I splashed cold water on my face, just to make sure I was awake. After that, I pulled on the cleaner of the two sets of clothes from yesterday. The other set would have to soak before getting washed.

You know exactly what I'm talking about. This whole nightmare could have been avoided. All the confusion. And the speculation on the part of your brother-in-law. I fear he believes you are crazy.

I let out a heavy sigh. "No thanks to you, I'm sure." Something niggled at the back of my mind. Hadn't there been something about this Voice in my dream? Something unpleasant? The brief image of a hooded man flashed behind my eyelids as I blinked. There was something sinister under that hood but I didn't want to think about it.

He would have found another reason to believe so.

Ha. Like that was possible. "You're wrong," I replied. I did a quick check to make sure I hadn't done anything stupid, like mismatching my buttons.

Am I?

Why did this Voice always have to be so adamant about everything? "I don't need you," I answered.

Don't you?

I didn't answer. Instead, I left the bathroom, almost running into Ron. He was standing just outside the doorway. I'm sure he was doing it on purpose. I wondered how long he'd been there but was too upset to consider what that might mean.

In the kitchen, Allisa was trying to help Russell pour a bowl of cereal. Somehow she managed to upend the entire box onto the table, getting only a small part into the too large bowl. I went to rescue the situation before it got any worse, exchanging the bowl for a smaller one.

Five minutes later, I had the two little monsters munching happily away on toasted fruit circles. And I had cleaned up most of the mess. I didn't realize until after I'd switched out the bowls that they'd somehow managed to spill half a gallon of milk on the floor. I found this out when my bare feet hit the white liquid and I made a spectacular dive for the floor, knocking my head into the table. Definitely not cool.

I saw stars for a good couple of minutes; long enough for Ron to do whatever it was he was doing in the bathroom. And even though there was a small lump on the side of my head, I decided to ignore it. It wasn't any worse than the headache I already had, or so I told myself.

I played with my cereal, pushing the colored loops around with my spoon. Ron sat down next to me. His face was clean-shaven and reeked of aftershave. I don't even know why they made that scent because it definitely was skunk worthy. "And how are we this morning," he inquired as he reached for the box of cereal. I wished he'd sit somewhere else, like in some kind of nose bleed section. Or that there'd be a bug in his cereal.

"I'm fine. As for you, I couldn't say." I turned to help Russell with his spoon. He was using the utensil to fling soaked circles around the kitchen. The distraction was a welcome one.

I felt Ron's sigh more than I heard it. He obviously didn't like my attitude. "You might win more friends if you'd be more cooperative," he commented. What he really was saying was that he wished I'd be more cooperative with *him*. Wasn't happening.

"I heard you talking to someone in the bathroom," he announced. Who knew if he'd actually heard what was being said. I had used the fan, after all. But that definitely proved that he'd been eavesdropping. Probably on purpose.

"What of it? Everyone does stuff like that. Some people even sing in the shower," I reminded him. "What does it matter to you if I'm talking to someone on the phone while using the john?"

He raised his eyebrows a bit. "Don't you think the phone cord is a bit short to reach the bathroom?" He looked at the kitchen phone. It was an old-fashioned one with a five-foot cord.

I glared at him. "Haven't you heard of cell phones?"

Ron pulled his own cell phone out and waved it in my face. "Where's yours?"

I chose not to answer. Besides, he knew I didn't have one. Or he was at least guessing that I didn't. I mean, I didn't have one up at the cabin, not that anyone got reception up there anyway. All the same, how could a college freshman afford something like that?

"Look," I turned to face him head on, "my business is none of your business, okay? So why don't you go analyze a toad or something?" I left the table, leaving behind a bowl of soggy little blobs.

Sara entered the kitchen as I was leaving. I heard Ron mutter something about my being difficult to her as she poured a bowl of fruity cardboard. I didn't hear her response because I slipped out the back door. I'd probably only retaliate in a less than awesome way.

I went over to my car and opened the passenger side door, rummaging around for my duffle bag. If I'd known what was good for me, I'd have just gotten in and driven off right then. But something held me back. I'm not sure what, but the universe wasn't done messing with me yet.

I closed the car door and slumped to the ground. This wasn't how things were supposed to go. This was not where I belonged. The mountains had somehow changed everything. Even if what I'd experienced had been just a dream. Because there was no way it had been real, as convoluted and twisted as the entire thing had been. It just wasn't possible. What was wrong with me?

After a while, I decided I'd wallowed enough in self-pity and headed back inside. The day was far from over. I still had to pack up my stuff.

Mom caught me as I entered the family room. She held up the backpack I'd been wearing at the cabin. I'd almost forgotten about it. "You left this in the van," she explained, handing it over. She leaned to one side, possibly checking out my goose egg. But if she saw actually it, she made no comment, which was weird. Maybe my hair hid it well enough from sight. Who knows?

"Uh, thanks," I said, accepting the bag as she left the room. I guess she was distracted by the loud crashing sound that came from the kitchen.

To be honest, I didn't remember ever having a bag like that. It was one of those leather ones where it's been so tanned that it almost feels like silk. There were several small pockets on the outside, with a larger pocket inside. And in that larger pocket was a book. My fingers caressed the familiar faded cover.

Just inside the cover of the book was an emerald green feather. It was just like the one from my dream. The one Christoph had pinned to his hat the first day I met him. But that wasn't possible. I held the feather up to my face, letting the loose fibers tickle my cheek. He had been a dream. Only a dream. But man did I wish he were real!

David invaded the room before I had a chance to examine the book. I shoved it back into the bag and closed it. There was no way I could deal with this right now. I mean, this book wasn't supposed to exist. At least not outside my dreams. That and my head wanted to explode.

"What have we there," David asked, taking the bag without asking.

"Give it back!" I demanded as I reached for it.

He held the pack out of reach. "It's so heavy. What've you got in here? Bricks?"

"Maybe," I hedged. Not even I was sure what all was in there. "Maybe it's my childhood rock collection. Now give it back." Why did my brother have to be such a pain?

David looked skeptical. "In a leather bag I've never seen before? Yeah right. Where'd you get it?" He began to fiddle with the top clasps.

"Mom!" I called out. That would stop him if nothing else would.

He pushed the bag at me. "Fine. If you're going to be such a baby about it, just take it."

I took it and shoved it in the space between the couch and the wall, shooting him a dirty look. No wonder he was still single. He had no respect for other people's privacy.

After I'd finished packing up my belongs, minus the help of nosy siblings, I took it all to the car. The leather backpack was snuggled between my sheet and my laundry. I saw Ron peeking out the front window and wondered what theories were cooking in his head now. Probably something like schizophrenia.

I popped the trunk, throwing my stuff inside the cramped space. It sure would have been nice if I could afford something more than this junk heap of a car. But at least it ran. I leaned against the closed trunk and sighed.

Why did I feel such a sense of disembodiment? It was like I was trying to bridge a gap between two different worlds. There was a slight nagging feeling that I didn't belong here. But then, hadn't I always felt that? Why should it come up again now?

Wonderful. This was the last thing I needed. I couldn't believe I was trying to analyze myself. Maybe I really was insane.

You have every right to feel this way, my Voice interposed. *They are not your blood relations. As such, it isn't really something to wonder at.*

"Oh, Puleeze," I told the Voice. "I've heard you say something like that before. Besides, I thought I told you to leave me alone."

Then maybe you are crazy. Crazy to not accept my help.

And where had his help gotten me? Nowhere. Except… but no. That had all just been a dream. He'd told me not to go yesterday. But he knew I would. Since when did I start referring to my Voice as "he", I wondered. Even though it was masculine, I'd always just called it "my Voice".

"I need more sleep," I told the air as I pushed away from my car and walked around to the driver's side. "And I'm not crazy."

CHAPTER SIXTEEN

A WEEK PASSED. A RATHER uneventful week at that. Ron stayed away from my college apartment. I'd have lost it if he hadn't. As things stood, my classes were more than doing the job. I wanted to pull my hair out because of the massive amount of assignments my teachers gave me. I had no time to worry about Ron, or whether anything had happened in the mountains or not.

That weekend, I stared at my biology homework. I'd read the same page at least three times now and decided I wasn't getting anywhere. With a heavy sigh, I pushed the stupid book aside. Getting up to stretch, I noticed the leather backpack I'd just thrown in the corner. It beckoned to me, like a twinkling light in the darkness.

Since trying to study wasn't getting me anywhere, I figured I had nothing to lose. I pulled the bag over and parked it on my bed. My fingers tingled as I opened the main pouch. I felt nervous for some reason, though I wasn't sure why. I had to wipe my hands on my quilt to get the sweat off.

All but shaking, I pulled the book out. It was just a plain, ordinary book! Why did I have to get all worked up over something so silly? It's not like there was anything earth shattering in there. And even if it was the same book from my mountain dream, the pages would just be blank. There was no reason for me to be anxious.

Slowly, almost as if I was waiting for something to jump out at me, I opened the cover, exposing the first page. I sighed with relief. The page was blank. I had nothing to worry about after all.

Deciding to make sure, I turned to the next page and stared. I felt like something had slipped into place, something crucial. Like a number on a combination lock. And right there, on the page, in my own handwriting, I read the following words:

> *I rolled over, aiming to hit the snooze button on my alarm clock. The insistent sound jarred my brain awake. But instead of finding the button, I felt myself falling, falling in slow motion.*

Crap. This couldn't be happening. My hands shook as I moved to turn several pages at once, accidentally turning more than I'd intended. There was no way this was possible.

> *So, could you tell me if this is reality or some psychotic dream I'm having? Because the last thing I remember is walking in a dark wood where it was raining, not snowing. And if this is some psychotic dream, could you please direct me to the nearest exit?*

I almost slammed the book shut, my heart pounding. What in the name of all sanity was this! This was, in no way, possible! But, of course, I had to be stupid. I grabbed the book and opened it up to somewhere near the second half.

He wore a tunic-like shirt over dark breeches, also green. He had a cap on his head with an emerald-green feather sticking out from the side, like a hatpin. He reminded me of the painting I'd seen back at the castle, the Robin Hood one I noticed my first night there. The eyes were similar, but more alive.

Crap! Crap! Crap! Crap!

I closed my eyes and saw the brief image of myself sitting down at the desk from the castle. I was writing something with a long quill pen. Trying to focus more on that image, I realized what I was seeing was me writing the same book I held in my hands. But when? How? This wasn't possible! All the events from the Waymeet came swirling into my head like a storm.

And so you finally begin to remember.

I opened my eyes in a flash, half expecting to see the hooded man, Kishan, standing in front of me. "You."

See? You do remember. He was laughing at me. And I hated it with every particle of my being.

"You are the reason I'm in this mess, aren't you," I demanded. "Why don't you just leave me alone?"

But if I did that, you'd never understand the full truth, now would you? And that would just be tragic.

I definitely did not trust his insincere sincerity. After all, if everything I was remembering was right, he was a dark wizard. Not only that, but he was bent on destroy me, and that was definitely not a good thing. Even though I knew this, I couldn't help but rise to his bait. "And why's that?"

Why, then you'd never know what happened to your mother. Your real mother. Kishan said the last part with an angry tone.

For whatever reason, I'm sure he would have liked nothing more than to hunt down my mother and kill her.

Then eat her soul. Or whatever it was he did to the souls he claimed.

"What does my Mom have to do with any of this?" I asked, sounding alarmed. I only knew one mother, and that was the one who'd raised me. But then, hadn't I always wondered if she wasn't someone else?

How does someone inherit green eyes from a family with blue ones? Those of my siblings who didn't have blue eyes had brown ones. And then the hair? How did I get dark auburn hair with a family full of blondes? Unless I wasn't genetically related, which meant that everything I'd grown up believing was a lie.

Kishan laughed in my mind. *See? Isn't it much more fun this way? Shall we see what happens next? Shall I tell you? No, I think not. Let's see if you can discover the truth on your own.*

The idea that what Kishan kept hinting at was true made my stomach churn. I tried to push the feeling away but couldn't. It made me a bit nauseous, to be honest. But now that the seed was firmly planted, there was no going back. I had to find out.

Without so much as a backwards glance, and stupidly leaving the book open on my bed, I dashed out of the dorm. I all but flew to my car. I would have driven over the speed limit to get to my parent's house, but my car wouldn't go any faster. Stupid heap of junk.

<hr>

There weren't any cars in the driveway when I arrived. And no one answered the door when I knocked. Was luck with me? I hoped that was the case as I located the key they kept hidden for emergencies. Dan locked himself out a lot. And who knew when one of us older siblings might need to break in for some reason or another? Siblings. Where they really my siblings?

Knowing where my parents kept the important documents, I headed straight for the basement. My dad had a small office down there. And tucked inside a steel filing cabinet, I found the file filled with the papers I was looking for. Birth certificates. Government identity cards. Everything.

I riffled through the papers, looking for any scrap that might tell me something. I couldn't find my birth certificate. But I did find something else, a birth certificate for another child named Emily. And a certificate of death dated one month later, on the day I celebrated my birthday. And then I saw what I'd been looking for; something I knew was there. It was a certificate of adoption with my name on it. Only there was no last name. Just Kas Lee. Was Lee my real last name?

I sat back as I held the paper in front of my face, as if holding it closer would somehow make it change. My eyes wouldn't focus on the words and I felt tears begin to prick behind my now closed eyelids. Everything had been a lie. Why didn't they tell me?

"You are not who you think you are."

Those words filled my mind as I cried. How right Milord had been when he'd said that. Had he known? And if so, why hadn't he told me? The only thing I could claim as my own was my name.

I don't know how long I sat there, but the next thing I remember was the sound of the back door closing. "Hello?" Mom. Great. "Kas? Are you here?"

Why did my Mom have to have such timing? "I'm downstairs," I called, knowing she'd start searching the house if I didn't answer. I put the adoption certificate down in an obvious location, right in front of me on the floor. I tried to wipe my eyes free of tears as I heard her footsteps coming down the stairs.

"I thought you had a major test to study for," Mom said as she entered the office. She stopped, seeing the paper in front of me. I could tell she was having a hard time keeping a straight face.

"When were you going to tell me?" I asked, pointing at the certificate.

I could see her swallow as she took in my tear-streaked face. But she just stood there and said nothing.

I tried again. "When were you going to tell me I was adopted?" I spoke slowly so there was no chance of her mishearing me. I could feel fresh tears just waiting to leak out. "Tell me."

Mom bent down and picked up the paper. Carefully, she put it back in the file and closed the drawer, her back to me. "It was Emily," she said. I could hear tears in her voice. "She was a beautiful baby, but something was wrong with her heart. She didn't live more than a month. I was devastated. Your father was devastated."

I couldn't say anything. I'd never seen, or heard, Mom cry before. Yell, yes. Cry, no. I had no idea how to deal with this development.

She turned around as she sniffled. "We couldn't bring ourselves to tell anyone. We only named her in the hope that she'd live. No one else knew, though. Because we knew she wouldn't."

Her words tore into me like barbs. I wanted to stop her from talking but didn't. I had to know.

"And then they took her away," Mom sobbed, reliving the moment she'd lost her child. "I knew I couldn't stand it. But then a woman came to see me. She said my name had come up as a potential candidate to adopt a special little girl."

I saw the image of a woman flicker before my eyes. She looked like Jenny, only older. She was explaining to my Mom about a child that needed a good family. A child whose mother could not keep her. Me.

Mom looked at me with pleading eyes. "It was like having my life given back to me. You became my baby. My Kas." She looked like she needed a tissue but I didn't have any to give her. "We both decided it was best to not tell you, or anyone else. David and Sara were young enough that they probably don't remember. They'd never seen Emily because she'd always been in the hospital."

"Never?" My ears filled with a low pitched buzzing sound that seeped into my brain. "Never tell me that I wasn't really a part of your family? That I didn't really belong?" My entire body tingled like I'd stuck my finger in an electrical socket.

I guess Mom could tell that her answer wasn't good enough. "It didn't seem to matter. We had you. We loved you, as if you were our own."

Platitudes. That's all her words were. Platitudes. Ways of making themselves feel better about what they'd done, or chosen not to do. My own parents, but no. Not my parents. Who was I, really?

I stood and moved towards the stairs, brushing her reaching arms aside. I staggered up the steps, feeling like I was blind. Out the back door. I don't know if Mom followed me or not.

I made my way to my car and slid behind the steering wheel. Was it forever my lot to be stuck between two realities? I wished for a mental breakdown, but that didn't happen. It sure would have made things easier.

Instead, I almost mechanically started my car and drove back home. To my home at the dorms. Why I didn't run into someone else's car, or run someone off the road is beyond me. But, somehow, I made it back without any problems. Once there, I crashed in bed, not wanting to move ever again.

We were riding, galloping across a wide-open field, Beauty and I. I wasn't sure if it was twilight or dusk. What I did know was that we were racing, urgently running into the darkness. And behind us streamed a host of hooded men on black horses. I wasn't sure if they were chasing us or trying to beat us in some mad race.

"You are the only one who can stop him."

Wolves. They were ravenous wolves. Not men. How could I have ever mistaken them for men?

Beauty reared on her hind legs. I clung to her mane. And then we were falling. Falling…

Onto the floor. My funny bone banged against the bed's frame and I winced. Then my arm went numb. I wanted to cuss, but didn't. It was definitely not my idea of the nicest wake up call. What a dream!

Then I remembered the face of that quack doctor, the one with the brandy for pain. Whatever had happened to him anyway? Unexplained mirth bubbled up inside of me. I laughed until I couldn't breathe. The tears just streamed down my face. I was surprised my roommate didn't come barging in to see what was going on. And the funny thing is I wasn't even sure why I was laughing.

Fifteen minutes later, I was still gasping for breath. It took another half hour to breathe normally again. After that, it took another hour to fall back to sleep. I don't remember dreaming anything else.

CHAPTER SEVENTEEN

THE NEXT COUPLE OF MORNINGS I felt numb. I went through the motions of going to school, of working. But it was like I was a zombie or something. I didn't know what to think or what to believe. I ate, slept, worked, and walked to and from my classes. That was it.

On the third morning, I seemed to wake from my stupor. It was enough to realize that even though I knew I was no longer who I thought I'd been, there were other possibilities. And all of those possibilities might be in that book. The weird book that I had somehow written without remembering I'd written it.

After searching my room for a good hour, I finally found the book on my computer desk. Which was weird because I was sure I'd left it on my bed, open. But then again, three days had passed. And if you'd asked me to recall a thing from any of those days, I wouldn't have been able to answer. It was possible I'd moved the book and just couldn't remember doing so. Or that someone had come snooping. I hoped not.

I found the backpack stuck between my bed and the wall. It had probably fallen there some time after I'd come home from my fake parents' house. I couldn't bring myself to think of them as my real parents anymore. Somewhere out there, my real parents waited. That, or they were dead. There was no way for me to know for sure. I didn't even know where I really came from.

My hands shook as I picked up the book and turned the thick pages. Even though it was a school day, I was determined to read as much as possible before something else happened. Maybe it covered what was going to happen, though I somehow doubted that. That would make things far too easy.

I got about five pages in, barely far enough to read about how David had slugged me on my way out of the bathroom. I was about to turn to the next page when something fell out from between the stiff sheets. Confused, I bent to pick up the folded paper I'd seen drop.

It was old, parchment I think. It was kind of yellowed, with an almost marble-like look to the whole thing. And it was thick, thicker than the pages of my book. The paper was folded twice. Maybe it was really some kind of leather. I wasn't sure. It felt smooth, not like regular paper. I unfolded it with great care, knowing that this somehow might reveal my fate. Even so, my hands shook as I smoothed out the folds.

This is to certify that, on this day, the twelfth of the thirteenth month of Rultari, Kas Lee ______, was born to our Lady, Jenesa, and our Lord, Dantol, through direct decent of the Royal Line. And is hereby declared the sole heir to the Rultan throne and all

I had to stop reading. Slowly, I lowered the paper and put it down on the desk. I stared at it without seeing it. The words seemed to be burned into the insides of my eyelids. On this day. Royal Line. Sole heir. How could this be possible? Was it some kind of joke?

The phone rang and I jumped. I stared at the thing as it vibrated next to the book. I saw the name on the caller ID and just stared. After a minute, the phone stopped making noise. Only to start ringing again less than a minute later. I guess Mom wasn't willing to talk to the voice mail. With a sigh, I hit the "talk" button, putting it on speaker.

"Honey?" Mom's voice came over the line, loud and clear. "I haven't heard from you for a while. Are you okay?"

I couldn't answer. What could I say? She probably didn't even know about this other certificate. I wasn't even sure where it had come from. But those first few sentences had changed everything. And now, my upside down world had come crashing down all around me.

"Are you there?" She sounded concerned. Maybe she wondered if I'd accidentally answered without realizing I'd done so.

I closed my eyes and let out a sigh. "Yes. I'm here," I said, my voice somewhat strained. I had to clear my throat. "Sorry. What was the question?"

Mom gave a somewhat exasperated sigh in return. "Honey, we're worried about you. You haven't answered any of our calls. It's not like you. Why don't you come home where we can talk?"

I blinked a few times, tears forming in the corners of my eyes. I wiped them away. "Home?" I sounded like a lost puppy.

"At least talk to someone. Ron, for instance. He might be able to help."

How could he help? He already thought I was crazy. He'd just lock me up and lose the keys. I couldn't. I wouldn't.

I'm sure Mom could sense my stubbornness over the line. "I want you to talk to Ron. If nothing else, he might be able to help you come to terms with all this. Or refer you to someone who can."

Yeah right. As if that was possible. I wanted to ask her if she'd leave me alone if I gave in. but I didn't. She'd be hurt by a comment like that. And, though she wasn't my biological mother, she had raised me. I didn't want to hurt her. After all, she'd thought she was doing the right thing by keeping me in the dark all these years. Even if her reasons weren't the best.

"Fine. I'll talk to him." Let the guillotine fall.

"Wonderful!" She seemed to perk up like a flower that had just been watered. "He said he could fit you in tomorrow afternoon. Meet him here, okay?"

Fit me in. He could fit me in. Wonderful. Exactly what families were for, right? I hung up the phone, forgoing the proper goodbyes. I felt so wanted. Not.

"There will be many whose paths will cross yours. They may well try to convince you that none of this happened, that it could not have happened."

I could hear Milord's voice loud and clear, as if he were standing next to me. Part of me wanted to turn around and look for his shadow, but I knew it was too good to be true.

I picked up the birth certificate and placed it between the last pages of the book. This... These pages would remind me of who I really was, and where I'd been. It would become my anchor.

And it will destroy you.

I would have laughed if I hadn't felt a sense that Kishan might be right about that. Maybe not physically, but mentally. After all, I had to go up against Ron. And this book was my only real proof that something more had happened. That and the feather. I knew those things wouldn't "fool" him, though

"You won't win, Kishan. I won't let you," I told him as I picked the book up again and started reading. He would not have the last word.

I read into the night, reliving the past half-year, committing it to memory. I would put my trust in the existence of Milord, Christoph, and Jenny. They were my strength. I just hoped that it would be enough.

Morning came way too early. Even though I'd stayed up all night reading, I still hadn't finished so I skipped my classes again. I read and paced. Read and paced some more. This process went on for hours. I even skipped lunch and dinner.

Every now and again I would take out the birth certificate. I could only assume it was real. The paper was just too old, the ink too brown with age, for it to be a fake. And then there was the golden seal. It depicted a creature so fantastical that it couldn't have been made up. I wasn't even sure what it was. I doubted it would sway Ron, but at *I* was convinced.

<hr>

Time moved on. Morning was almost gone and I would have to leave soon. I didn't want to go, but I'd agreed. What had I gotten myself into? I wasn't sure, and that alone made me feel that I would regret it.

I sat on my bed and played with the emerald-green feather, running it down my cheek again and again. The bag was on the bed, sitting near the edge. I'd thought about rummaging in it but hadn't because there was just so much to read, to remember. I looked at the clock. Time to go.

Standing up, I accidentally knocked the backpack to the floor. I heard something metallic hit the hard wood. I bent to pick up whatever had caused that sound. It was a long gold chain with a green stone hanging from it. I'd worn that stone before. It was part of the ensemble they'd put me in that first night in Mantaset. It went perfectly with the gaudy green dress I'd shunned, and those stupid high heeled shoes.

I held the faceted stone tightly in one hand until it began to get warm. I closed my eyes, breathing in a word of thanks and hoped Milord could hear it. He had to have been the one to put it there. Or had Jenny put it there? I knew she wouldn't have thought about it on her own.

I put the chain around my neck and let the stone hang down underneath my shirt. It was time to face my fate. I just hoped this stone meant Milord would protect me, even if it was only a thought of fancy.

CHAPTER EIGHTEEN

THE DRIVE OUT TO MY parents' house was uneventful. It passed too quickly. It didn't go by fast enough. I didn't know which was worse.

Ron's car was already in the driveway. I noticed that my parent's van was not. I checked my watch and groaned. I was late, maybe only by five minutes, but I knew he'd note that down. He always wrote everything down. I could see him peeking out the front window. When he opened the front door, I decided my original intent of using the backdoor was a fail. He would be waiting for that. Besides, he'd already seen me. So much for that idea.

"I've been waiting for you," Ron said without preamble. "You're late."

I pushed past him and went for the only couch Mom kept in the front room. "Traffic," I answered, trying to communicate as little as possible. "I couldn't justify running red lights or stop signs. I'm sure you understand."

He wasn't amused. Maybe it had something to do with my tone. How could my sister, er adopted sister, ever have fallen for him? It was a truly inconceivable notion to me. Just what was wrong with everyone? The guy was a creep! He followed me inside, after closing the door behind us.

I noticed he locked the door. This should be fun, I thought. He then proceeded to explain to me that everyone else had gone out somewhere so that we wouldn't be interrupted. I'd already guessed but still didn't like the idea. I was at his mercy. Unless I could run, which would look really, really bad.

Since I'd already taken over the couch, he took up the armchair facing opposite my perch. I think he locked the door to slow me down if bolted. A coffee table between us, which I thought was nice. If he decided to become physical in any way, I had something we could dance around, literally and figuratively.

He pulled out a little notebook and a voice recorder, which he turned on. Didn't he have to ask permission or something? This wasn't official. He couldn't ethically analyze me, after all. Wasn't what he was doing called entrapment or something?

"Now, Kas, I want you to understand that I'm only doing this as a favor to help you. Your mother mentioned that you've been under a lot of pressure lately. Especially since you just learned about being adopted."

I could imagine him being a bit gleeful about that one. That kind of situation was bound to cause mental havoc in even the most sane of people. And to say that I'd been under a lot of pressure lately? That was the understatement of the century, not that he knew that. And he didn't need to know that. But I knew he would do his level best to try and get whatever he'd come for. I had to be on my guard.

Ron cleared his throat and made a few notes. Who knows why. "Learning you were adopted, after all this time, must have been difficult. How did learning this make you feel?" He looked up, waiting.

I didn't know if I dared answer. I didn't know if I could. I'm sure my distress showed on my face. He could easily read that if he wanted. But he wasn't going to be content with just that. "You felt betrayed, didn't you?"

My more belligerent side decided to come out. "Are you asking me if that's how I felt? Or are you trying to feed me what you think I should be feeling?"

Ron leaned forward, probably trying to go for a more "intimate" feel. If so, he failed miserably. I'd never liked him and I would never trust him. "I can't help you if you won't let me. If you won't answer for your sake, then please answer for your mother's."

I felt like rolling my eyes but knew that would go down in his notes. I wasn't there for me. Mom just kept pestering. I also knew he'd keep pressing until I admitted something though. And I had no idea how long Mom and dad were going to be gone. If I just up and left, he'd use that as an excuse to schedule another time. It was now or never. "Yes, I felt betrayed, okay?"

Ron smiled as he jotted that down. "Good," he replied. "We're making some progress. Why did you feel betrayed?"

I raised my brows, wondering if he was kidding me. That one should have been obvious. I decided to try and turn the tables on him. "How would you feel if you just found out that you weren't who you thought you were? That you were lied to your entire life?"

He pushed up his glasses. "Do you feel like you were lied to?" Of course he'd find a way to turn it back on me.

"What do you think," I almost spat, but caught myself just in time.

He sighed, as if he were trying to exercise patience. "It's not important what I think. What's important is what you think. Why don't you tell me?"

Could have fooled me, I thought as I stood up. "Yes, okay?" I felt the floodgates open. "I mean, I knew I wasn't like anyone else in my family. But learning that they'd deliberately hidden that I wasn't biologically theirs..." I caught myself before I could continue, and then dropped back down on the couch. Now I'd done it.

Ron was writing again. He didn't look up as he continued with his questions. I think he was doing it on purpose to unnerve me."And how long have you felt misplaced?"

"All my life," I gave in with a sigh. Hopefully he would stick to that topic. It was far safer than any of the others he could pull out.

He kept his pen poised as he looked up over the rim of his glasses. "And how long have you been hearing voices?"

I should have known. That was, of course, the main reason he'd volunteered to try and help me out. It had to be. Then he could make me into some kind of case study, become rich and famous or something like that. But I had to keep this to myself. There was no way I could tell him. "Excuse me?"

Ron tapped the pen on his notebook. He was definitely expecting something more. "Remember the morning we all went up to your grandfather's cabin?"

Clearly he didn't associate himself with most of my family. Yeah. He was one of those types. Even though he technically married into the family, he only associated with them because of Sara. If it hadn't been for her strong sense of family, I'm sure he would have convinced her to move to some remote location. My vote would have been for Dansveld, clear on the other side of the planet.

And even though he was trying to direct things, I wasn't about to let him have his way. "What about that morning? It had been a rough week at work. I woke up on the wrong side of the couch. No big deal."

He raised his eyebrows at me and clicked his pen closed before folding his arms. Couldn't get that white shirt stained, after all. "You know exactly what I'm talking about. You tried to convince your mother to give you a pass on the birthday celebration. When she asked why, you told her that your little voice told you not to go."

I nodded, like I was catching on to a bad joke. "Oh. That. Well, you see, that's a code of mine that I've used for years to tell Mom I'm not feeling well." I deliberately used the more personal name for my adopted mother, hoping he'd realized he was being a you-know-what. I don't think he got the hint.

Ron crossed his legs. "So, you're trying to tell me that you and your mother use a special code to communicate so that others don't know what's going on?" He definitely sounded skeptical. Besides, if he chose to believe that, it would throw a wrench in his potential case study options. Unless he was looking at other possibilities.

I shrugged. "Sorry to disappoint," I replied, not sorry in the least. I tried to keep the smugness from my tone. Who knew what he'd make of that. I began tapping my fingers against my knees, wondering just how much longer this stupid game would go on. I mean, it's not like I didn't have better things to do, because I did. I still had a lot to read in that book. And I hadn't completely explored the contents of that backpack yet. Yeah, lots still to do.

Ron decided to switch tactics. I could see the gleam of challenge in his eyes. "What if I were to tell you that your mother has already confirmed that you have spoken to voices all your life? Would that make you change your answer?" He recrossed his arms and stared at me.

I stared right back at him. "I'd say you're lying." Chances were good that Mom had not said anything like that to him, though it wasn't impossible. I mean, if Mom thought my hearing a voice was somehow connected to my behavior now, things didn't bode well for me.

Just as I have tried to tell you.

Oh great. Again? Kishan's timing was horrible. I wanted to groan but didn't. That would give myself away and I wasn't going to do that. Not in front of Ron. And if I tried to explain to him that the Voice I'd heard my entire life belonged to a dark wizard who wanted to destroy me?

Well, let's just say that the men in white coats would all but jump out of the woodwork. So, I decided to ignore him.

Ron cleared his throat. "Kas? Would that make you change your answer?"

I rolled my eyes, feeling the frustration building. "Okay, if you want to play that game, fine. Hypothetically, if what you'd said was true, I might answer with a sure. That changes everything. Let me tell you about the strange masculine voice that I've heard my entire life because I'm some kind of crazy psychopath. Not only that, but the little voice that I hear is trying to kill me. Would that make you happy?"

Clearly I had said something to make him take a step back. I could see him mentally retreating a few steps. Well, it was nice to be on the offensive for once. I'm sure it would cost me later though.

"Why don't you tell me about this Milord you mentioned at the cabin?" he suggested. Definitely a different track now. I guess he didn't like where the other one was going.

Was this guy for real? "You want me to talk about some guy I mentioned from a dream over a week ago? Are you serious? It was a dream, okay? Weird things happen in dreams."

I guess Ron thought he'd gotten back on track because he picked up his notebook and clicked open his pen. "Why don't you tell me about your recent dreams?"

I could tell he didn't believe me. Well, it wouldn't hurt to be a bit more truthful. "Haven't slept much lately. I'm sure you understand why. I mean, finding out I've been lied to my entire life seems to have that kind of effect, you know?"

I could see Ron chewing on the inside of his lip. That was a bad habit I hoped he'd lose. It looked downright weird. "I can see that you're not going to be cooperative."

I heard Kishan laughing and wondered what was so funny. I felt my heart thud in my chest. It was so strong that it almost hurt. I closed my eyes and realized I felt the green stone pressing against my skin under my shirt. Was it my heart pulsing so hard, or was it the stone?

I felt something like an electric charge course through me. My eyes opened wide. My mind opened wider. And I remembered.

"If you harm her—"
"Careful, princeling, wouldn't want to lose your temper would you? What would your subjects say?"

I suddenly realized who'd spoken those words. Kishan and Milord. Even back then, Milord was looking out for me, protecting me.

"I have been with you the entire time. I never left."

I could hear Milord's voice as if he were sitting next to me. I had to resist the urge to look over, afraid of what I would or wouldn't see.

But he was always watching over me. From the shadows where I couldn't see him. Was that why I couldn't see him? Not because of the rules of the Waymeet, but because that was how he wanted things to be? Because he protected me better from within the shadows? Was that how it worked?

I *watched over you.* I *protected you*, Kishan protested. *You owe me your life!*

My mind was too caught up in the realization to give the wizard much thought. Besides, he almost sounded like Russell throwing a tantrum. I always ignored those. I could feel him calling his followers to him.

I should have felt afraid, but I didn't. Somehow I knew he couldn't harm me here, not in this plane, not directly at least. It wasn't where he belonged. And I knew that hiding what had happened would only bring him closer. Hiding was not the answer.

Ron was staring at me, unmoving. In fact, the clock on the piano wasn't moving either. The hands were frozen as if time itself had stopped. And somehow, I was the one who had stopped it.

"It is a gift. Something you were born with. This, among many others."

I saw my mother. My *real* mother. Her auburn hair was lighter than mine, but her eyes were my own. Her skin was fair and she was smiling. I blinked and she was gone. I pressed a hand against my forehead, feeling a sudden pressure there.

"Are you alright?" I heard Ron ask. I saw him leaning forward as I looked up. His tone had become much more professional all the sudden.

I blinked a few times, trying to settle everything that had happened in just the blink of an eye. I couldn't hide this anymore, no matter how crazy Ron thought I was because of it. "I… I just saw my mother," I answered, still in shock.

Ron misunderstood. He glanced towards the window, expecting to see the van pulling back into the driveway.

"No." I looked at him, capturing his attention with the intensity of my expression. "I just saw my *real* mother."

He pinched the bridge of his nose, like he had a sudden headache or something. "I'm confused," he admitted. "What do you mean you just saw her?"

I stood and walked over to the window, looking out. I'd always loved looking out that window. The neighbors across the street had an orchard within easy view. In the spring, the pink and white flowers filled the whole area with a fragrant breeze. But, now, in autumn, the leaves were turning orange and red.

I clasped my hands behind my back and contemplated the view. "Have you ever wondered if there were more worlds out there than this? If there might be alternate planes of reality that we can't see?"

"You mean like waking, dream, and fantasy?" I could hear him scribbling again. I guess my calmer demeanor reassured him that I was more willing to cooperate.

I shook my head and turned around, hands still clasped behind my back. "No. More like inter-dimensional merging. Two existences overlapping into a neutral place to create an alternate plane of existence."

Ron was still confused. I could see it in his eyes. I'm sure he never expected to get an elementary physics lesson. He would never admit to it though. "And how does this relate to your mother?"

I moved over to the piano and sat on the bench. Pulling a few music books from the pile next to the instrument. "Suppose that this is us." I held up one book. "And that this," I held up another, "is a different dimension." I set them down on top of the coffee table where he could see them.

"If they reach out to each other," I continued as I opened up the cover of both books so they overlapped. "They cross into an area that doesn't belong to either of them, but to both of them."

I was amazed at how much this concept made sense, now that I'd had my moment of clarity. I wasn't sure why I hadn't gotten it before. It was so simple.

Ron leaned forward to examine what I'd done. He raised an eyebrow at the overlapping covers. But at least he wasn't scribbling notes. That meant he was paying attention.

"Now," I continued, "suppose that there's a planet out there that's like ours. What if it also reaches out and joins in that shared space?" I added another book, opening its pages to join the touching covers of the other two books. "You have a junction, a place that is but isn't. A bridge, if you will. And it spans all three realities or worlds. And you can keep adding in as many as you like, layer upon layer."

Ron was thinking, rubbing his chin. "And where did you learn about this phenomenon, or is it all made up to impress me?"

He wasn't getting it, even with the visual. I heard Kishan laughing at my efforts. "Milord taught me," I answered, confirming that I did, in fact, remember the supposed "dreams" from the cabin. I'm sure they were more of a memory than a creation of my mind.

He caught onto the fact that I'd lied. "I thought you'd told me you didn't remember dreaming about such a person. And how could someone who is only in your dreams instruct you on something like that?" He pointed at the books.

I sighed. It was now or never. Too bad I'd already confused the poor guy. I almost felt sorry for him. "How would you feel if someone you don't know or like comes up and starts asking you questions about something you have kept private? Delving into your most secret thoughts and hopes? How would that make you feel?"

I think my earnest tone threw him off guard because I could see the shock in his eyes. "I might react just as you have," he admitted after a few moments.

I inclined my head, accepting the sort of apology. "Then let me explain to you what you want to hear. Yes, I sometimes hear a voice. And I have heard it for as long as I can remember."

He began scribbling again, almost as if something were eating him up in inside. Chances were good he wasn't really taking in what I was telling him. His mind was too mechanical for that. I wondered if he ever felt anything besides disdain, the thrill of being proved right, or other similar emotions. If that were the case, I pitied him.

"What kinds of things does this voice tell you?" he asked, his pen still for the moment. I knew it would be flying across the notebook's pages a lot more before we were finished. In fact, I was kind of expecting him to just keep going without me talking.

I had to think about his question for a minute. For the most part, the Voice, Kishan's voice, had given good advice. Part of me wondered if his warnings weren't somehow connected to fabricated situations. But if that were the case, he'd been playing me along. Doing things to gain my trust without me even realizing his true nature.

"He used to tell me helpful things," I admitted. "When I told Mom, she called it my 'little guide'. I think she believed he was an imaginary friend. You'll have to ask her to be sure. But recently, I've decided to just ignore him."

Ron looked up from his notes. "So, is this voice the one you call Milord?"

I shook my head. "No. He'd like me to think he was, but he isn't. To be honest, I'd rather he disappear."

Ron nodded at that as he jotted down some more notes. "It's always good to admit you have a problem and want to fix it," he agreed, not realizing we were on two completely different pages. And maybe even two completely different books, in separate libraries.

We both looked up at the sound of a car driving on gravel. Mom and dad had returned. Allisa and Russell all but pushed their way out of the van. Dan was slower in following them. Mom and dad followed, both looking rather harried and worn out. No wonder they always made me watch Russell. They were tired after only a few hours.

I'm sure Ron would have pushed for a few more comments but wasn't able to do so because dad unlocked the back door. Ron never really liked dad, for some odd reason. He seemed to like David even less. Mom came in next, heading for the living room. "I'm sorry, Ron," she apologized. "We tried to stay longer but both of us were worn out at the park."

I'm sorry, Ron. No hello, Kas. Nothing. "Hello mother. How are you? I'm fine. Thanks for asking." I stood and left the room. I could see Mom's confusion as I brushed past her on my way to the back room. The front door was still firmly locked against me.

———

Somehow I knew they would start talking about me the moment I'd left so I opened and closed the back door, pretending to leave. I then tiptoed towards the stairwell, which shared a wall with the living room. There was a slight ledge against the wall where I could crawl, if I was careful. If not, I'd fall into the stairwell. I was careful.

"What was that all about?" I heard Mom ask as I pressed my ear up against the wall.

I could hear movement and assumed it was either Mom sitting or Ron gathering his things together. "I'm not sure," he answered. "After talking with her, I'm not sure what to make of the situation. It would be easy to call her delusional but I don't think that's the case. I think it runs much deeper than that."

There was silence for maybe a minute. Perhaps they were both thinking about what Ron had just said. At least I'm sure Ron was thinking about it, convincing himself his theories were correct. But that's all they were. Theories.

He cleared his throat. "Have you ever heard her voice? I mean the one that she says talks to her?"

I could answer that one for him, but that would give me away. Mom had never heard Kishan. Only I had. There was no need for her to hear him.

"No," Mom sighed. It was a loaded sigh. I didn't like the taste it left in the air.

"And how long have you known about this little voice?" he pressed. I wondered if he'd turned off his recorder or if it was still running.

Mom was thinking. I could tell. She always made little noises when she was thinking. "Since she was little. Maybe four or five?"

I'm sure if I'd been standing in the room with them, I'd have seen Ron rubbing his chin again. "An imaginary friend?" I knew where he was going with this.

"I'm not sure," Mom admitted. "I always thought of it as her guiding light."

More silence. Ron cleared his throat again.

"I think she's reaching out. Telling me I should have reached out to her more." Mom's words surprised me. I knew she loved me, but to think she felt like she'd failed me was something else entirely. None of this was her fault. It was never her fault.

"I think she's unstable." He would. Stupid Ron. And stupid Sara for marrying him. "Imaginary friends are not uncommon in children. But to carry them into adulthood is something else. It suggests a lack of connection with reality. And her descriptions of an alternate reality support my theory."

I could imagine Mom putting a weary hand to her head. I wouldn't blame her if she had a headache. If I were in her shoes, I would have had one too. "Alternate reality?"

"It's a story for another time," Ron said, brushing it aside. I'm sure he didn't want to get into it, or try to explain it. I doubt he'd be able to. "My advice to you is to have her brought in for observation for a while. We can proceed from there. If need be, she can be medicated or institutionalized."

Someone stood up. I heard the couch squeak.

"She's my daughter!" Yay for Mom!

"And she's ill," Ron interrupted. "Very ill. Now, I can't personally have her admitted anywhere because we're related. There's a matter of ethics." Oh, now it came out. How silly of him not to mention that in front of me, not that I hadn't already know that. "But I can ask a colleague for a second opinion. Should he agree with my analysis, he could have her brought in."

I didn't want to listen to any more of this. Listening to them discuss my potential fate. But I had to know what Mom would do. I strained my ears to hear everything, waiting while the woman who'd raised me debated my supposed future. I could hear Kishan laughing again.

"Alright," Mom gave in. "But you'll have a hard time convincing her to go anywhere, let alone see anyone else."

I heard Ron click his pen. He was probably putting it away. Finally. "If we have to, we can file a court order mandating it." He said that as cool and calculating as any super villain in a cheesy movie would. I knew there was a reason I didn't like him.

I couldn't make myself listen anymore. I crawled back to the landing and slipped out the back door. I would never be able to prove to them I was right. That I was sane. But I knew, beyond any shadow of a doubt, that I'd been where I had been. I'd heard what I'd heard. And seen what I'd seen. To deny that would be to deny myself, no matter what they said. I would not let them take me.

From looking at the sky, I could tell it was late afternoon. I'd been in there longer than I'd planned. And with this new development, I knew I didn't have a lot of time. Even though I apparently had the gift of manipulating time, I didn't know how to use it. But I knew Ron would not wait.

With Kishan's influence, I'm sure he was already making arrangements. It would not have surprised me if it had been Kishan who had set the whole thing up in the first place. If he could trap me here, he could keep me from my true destiny.

And now that I knew who I really was, I knew my destiny did not lie here. But if he could keep me here... I didn't want to think about that.

They would both try to trap me with time. Ron had the recording of our session. He could manipulate it in whatever manner he wanted. It wasn't necessary to have me actually see this colleague of his. Knowing Ron, he'd convince the guy to commit me without the luxury of actually meeting me.

And chances were good this colleague would be as like-minded, or at least was as easily manipulated. I was doomed. It didn't help that I was technically still a minor and therefore subject to the whims of the court. Joy.

CHAPTER NINETEEN

I GOT INTO MY CAR and started the engine. I hoped they thought I'd just been sitting out there the entire time. It would be bad if they knew I'd listened in to that last bit of conversation. I'm sure Ron would find a way to keep me there if he knew. That way I couldn't escape him and his master plan of ruining my life.

My but how easy it is to manipulate those who don't want to believe, Kishan commented with amusement. *I don't know why I didn't try doing this sooner.*

I put the car in gear and backed out of the driveway. "You won't win," I told him, pausing to shift gears so I could away.

Think what you will, princess, but I have already won. You don't yet know your full potential, or how to use your abilities. The gates of your prison are already closing. Your time is running out.

I all but spun out of the driveway getting onto the main road, pressing down on the gas pedal like I was playing one of those racing games. My tires screeched in protest. "You won't win," I reemphasized.

His laughter rang out. *I already have. They will detain you, ensnare you, and your true home will be mine. You will be powerless to stop me.*

His malice caused frost to creep up my windows. I turned on the defroster and kept going. I'd learned too much, been through too many things to give in.

I felt warmth spread between my ribs. I slowed down and pulled out the chain from under my clothes. The green gem was glowing. The light sent dazzling reflections off every surface in my car. I knew I was not alone.

He can't help you here.

Kishan was too quick with his words. He was scared. I could feel it. I mentally built up a barrier against him and his intrusions into my mind.

You can't shut me out!

"Watch me," I replied.

Another car came racing down the road behind me as I got back up to speed. It swerved like mad. I could feel Kishan's intent on it, drawing it closer. I stepped on the gas. The car behind me went faster. "What are you doing!"

The car was inching up alongside mine, even though we were on a typical two-lane country road. Whoever was driving that vehicle was on the wrong side of the street. I looked back and saw the driver. His eyes were vacant orbs as he stared straight ahead. Not good.

"Leave him alone!"

This is not your world. You can't order me around.

A coward. That's what Kishan was, nothing but a coward. And he was playing a deadly game with lives that weren't his own.

I saw a side street coming up. The car was already neck and neck with mine. I stepped off the gas. His car passed mine as I quickly turned down the new street.

No!

I knew Kishan's influence had left the driver. I could hear the squeal of brakes as he came back to his senses. I hoped he was okay but didn't go back to help. I didn't want to stop until I reached my dorm.

It took over two hours to get back. I'd gotten lost a few times, taking roads I wasn't familiar with. I would not let Kishan win. And believe me, he tried. But I made back to my dorm without any other major incidents. Milord was protecting me.

———

All the lights were off when I opened the door to my room. I didn't bother turning them on, preferring to stumble through the dark. My first stop was the blinking answering machine. I didn't have to hit the button to know whom at least one of those messages was from, but I wanted to be sure.

Beep.

"Kas, this is Mom. I just want to make sure you got home all right. Please call me."

Beep.

"Kas, this is Ron. I've mentioned you to a colleague of mine and he'd like to meet with you tomorrow. He just wants to ask a few questions, kind of a follow up to what we did today. Give me a call."

Beep.

"Kas, are you home? Your father and I are getting worried. I'm thinking about calling the police but he's told me to wait. I hope you talk to Ron's friend tomorrow. Call me."

I erased the messages. If I talked to Ron's friend, he'd have me at least put in an institution for observation. And, worse to worse, he'd have me institutionalized into forever, with Kishan's blessing. I couldn't allow that. I had to leave. Now. They must not find me. I would never meet with this friend, not even if the court ordered me to.

I slipped into my bedroom and turned on a small lamp, setting it on the ground. I didn't want any light to leak out of the closed curtains. Who knew if they were watching this place or not? With my luck, chances were good they were.

I pulled out the leather backpack and stuffed in the book. I added a few personal belongings as well. They might not seem important to most people, but to me they were to me. A stuffed animal I'd had since I was two. A snow globe grandpa had given me. A few photos.

Heading back to the kitchen area, I packed a few essentials. I included granola bars, a few sandwiches, water bottles, and some fruit snacks. I even remembered to put in a flashlight and some rope. I was ready.

But I couldn't leave yet. I couldn't leave without some explanation. I owed Mom that much. I sat at the table and took out some paper, contemplating what I wanted to write.

Dear Mom,

I may not have told you enough how much I love and appreciate you, but I do. I'm sorry if I have caused you any undue pain or worry. I now know who I am and where I came from. And while I appreciate everything you and dad have done for me. But I still have to do this.

Please understand that I am leaving only because I have to. My happiness depends on it. I know what Ron is planning and can't allow that to happen. I'm not crazy. I just have a different calling in life. I'm sorry if neither of you understand.
Please don't look for me. You won't find me.

I didn't know what else to write. How could I explain everything that had happened in a short letter? There wasn't any way possible. So I left off there, hoping she'd understand. Chances were good she wouldn't though.

I didn't fold the letter. I put it in the most obvious place, leaving it in the middle of the kitchen table. I was tempted to leave the green feather with it, but didn't. They wouldn't understand what it meant.

I took out my driver's license and debit card from my wallet, leaving the rest behind. I probably wouldn't need it, but it was better to have. Besides, I needed to fill up my car's gas tank. I knew it would leave a trail, but that would quickly grow cold. I only planned on using it once.

Now set on my path, I took off the key to my car from the key ring, leaving the others behind with everything else. I didn't even bother locking the apartment door as I left. It wouldn't hurt to make it a little easier on them. Besides, there was nothing left there that I didn't mind losing.

It was just before midnight by the time I went back to my car, making sure to clean out all the non-essential items. I stopped only to get gas, and then drove out of town.

I headed towards the mountains, driving carefully up the winding road. I thought my car would give out a few times from the steep incline, but it held out. There was no way I was walking the rest of the way.

I had to ditch my car at the bottom of the hill leading to the family cabin. It couldn't make the last climb so I left it in the small village nearby, among a group of other junkers. The hike would do me good. And, thankfully, it only took me half an hour to reach my destination. It took another half hour to figure out where the spare key was stashed. I let myself in. Locking the door behind me, and then lay down for a short rest.

Beep. Beep. Beep. Beep.

I groaned at the insistent sound of my watch alarm going off. But I got up and brushed out the wrinkles from the few hours of sleep I'd allowed myself. Not that sleeping on a crinkly sheet of plastic was really all that comfortable anyway. It was so early that the sun hadn't even risen yet. I stubbed my toes on the way to the bathroom, forgetting to grab my flashlight.

The water that came from the faucet was ice cold. It woke me up and set my teeth to chattering. My body complained about the lack of rest. My stomach complained about a lack of food. I ate one of the sandwiches I'd packed. Then I went in search of my flashlight, which I found under the bed.

With my stomach at least pacified, I folded the borrowed blanket from my plumber uncle's stash. Shouldering my bag, I locked the cabin door behind me. I returned the key to the same strut underneath the building where I'd found it. Then I headed into the woods, seeking out the Sitting Rock, where all this had started. Once there, I waited for the sun to rise.

With the first rays of light filtering through the trees, I pulled out the green stone. It was hard to not think of Milord and that first night I'd met him. Would I see him again soon? And what about Christoph? The idea made my heart thud almost painfully in my chest. I wanted to see them both with equal anticipation.

I wasn't sure how I'd gotten to the Waymeet in the first place, so I decided to try and reenact what had happened that afternoon. It was the only place where I knew to look for both of them. But would either of them still be there? Would either of them be reaching back for me?

Light continued to creep through the trees. I saw the beginnings of different colors fill the sky above me, first pink and then red. The sky was cloudless for as far as I could see, which wasn't all that far thanks to the trees. I closed my eyes and clung to the Rock, waiting for something to happen. Nothing did.

I stood up, determination in my stance. How did one open the gateway? I closed my eyes again, holding the green stone in one hand. I thought about the castle of Mantaset, the forest, and about the meadow. Still nothing.

"Milord!" I called out. "I'm ready! I want to come home."

That is not your home.

I opened my eyes, feeling ill. Kishan was there, standing only a few feet away. His dark hood was pulled low over his face, but I remembered what it looked like. "You."

"Did you think it would be that easy?" He laughed with disdain, sweeping his cloak with one hand. Drama queen.

The air looked odd around him, like some kind of intense heat was warping it. Except it wasn't hot. I heard car doors slam from somewhere near the cabin.

"Kas!"

"Kas?"

They were calling for me, voices I knew and didn't know. They were coming closer, drawn by Kishan. He would stop at nothing to stop me. I saw them through the trees as they followed the trail. Then they were standing in front of me. Mom. Dad. Ron. Sara. And some men I didn't know. One wore a suit. The others were in some kind of medical uniform.

"I give you a choice. Go back with them and live. Or try to press on and die. Either way, your dear Christoph will never see you again." Why couldn't I see his full face?

I blinked back my surprise. Yes I'd been thinking about them both. But how had Kishan known that my heart yearned more towards the one? "Christoph?"

"Stupid girl! Haven't you realized it yet? The man you call Milord? He is nothing more than a man, one who can be destroyed! And he has been charading this entire time!" Kishan's malice was palpable.

The last few pieces slipped into place at his words. Christoph was Milord. How had I not realized this before?

Their voices were identical. The same tenor tones. The same inflections, even though he'd tried to sound different. How had I been so blind? Except I hadn't. Part of me had known all along.

"You shall not have her."

Christoph. My heart burned. He was more than a just a man. He was my protector. My benefactor. And the man I loved.

"Kas, come home. Dr. Lewis can help you. You're not well," Mom called out to me from the path.

I looked at her. "Did you get my letter?" She didn't answer.

"Kas, you need help. Let me help you." Ron. Did he still not get it?

"Can you see him? Can you see Kishan? He's right there in front of you. Only a few feet away from me," I gestured.

"There's no one there." It was the man in the suit. He must be Dr. Lewis.

"They can't see me. They won't see me, unless I let them," Kishan gloated.

"Come with us and we can help you. We can take away all this confusion," Dr. Lewis said. I didn't like his voice. It was whiny. Like Ron's. I'm sure they would have loved to "help" me and take away my "confusion". With pills that would cause what they said they were curing. No way.

"Just put the gun down, Kas." Dr. Lewis was holding out his hand, like he was trying to convince a scared animal to let him touch it.

I was confused. Gun? "What are you talking about?"

Dr. Lewis didn't relax his stance. He had one knee bent just a little. It reminded me of a wild animal waiting to pounce. "Just put the gun down. Suicide is not the answer."

I looked at Kishan. His mouth was twisted in a cruel

smile. "I don't have a gun," I yelled back.

"But they see one in your hands," Kishan smiled. His teeth were disgusting. "Illusions are powerful tools. Wouldn't you agree?"

Illusions. He was using illusions. "They're not real," I accused. "They're not really here. You're just trying to trick me. It won't work. You've told me nothing but lies my entire life. I will have no more of it."

I charged at him, running as fast as I could. I squared my shoulders, like I'd seen professional athletes do. The moment I made contact with him, the world shattering, raining down like broken glass into nothing.

"Kas?"

I sat up with a jolt. It was dark. And I felt plastic underneath me. A rough blanket covered my body.

"Hey, it's okay. It's just me." It was David's voice. What was he doing here? I heard him strike a match. Then I saw his face as he lit a propane lamp.

"David," I sighed in relief. I pinched myself, just to be sure I wasn't still dreaming.

He smiled at me, his hair looking disheveled, like he hadn't bothered showering the day before. "Hey, sis."

I looked around and realized I was still in the cabin. Those moments with Kishan must have been a dream. Unless it had happened because we were that close to the Gateway. It was possible the universe was reaching out its many fingers into this reality.

"It's okay," David reassured as he sat down on the bed, right next to me. "You must have been dreaming. I thought I might find you here though. Mom's been frantic since last night. She even called the police. They all seem to think you've lost it or something." He laughed at the idea.

I gulped, not sure how to take this. "And you?"

He cuffed me on the shoulder. "Me? I've always known you were weird. But seriously, Ron wants you institutionalized. Not sure what you did to him, but he's definitely got it out for you. He looked almost rabid."

I sighed and pushed back the blanket. "All this over hearing a stupid Voice." I put my feet on the ground. "I heard him and Mom talking about it yesterday. But what are you doing here? And what time is it?"

David looked at his watch, making it light up to see the numbers. "It's just past five in the morning." He stood up. "And I'm making you breakfast." I noticed he'd brought a grocery bag, which I could just see over the kitchen counter. There's a lot to be said about open rooms.

"After hearing the news from Mom, I knew you'd try to retrace your steps," he explained as he moved towards the stove. "I tried to call you at your place but got no answer so I figured you'd make your way here. And I was right."

I didn't know what to say so I followed him into the kitchen area, watching him light the old gas stove with practiced ease. "You didn't tell anyone else, did you?"

David took out a pan and set it over the lit burner. "I didn't breathe a word to anyone. Promise. But I did get to hear Ron's spiel when he brought that Dr. Lewis over. He was all but foaming at the mouth when he talked to Mom. That's when I snitched their copy of the key and headed up."

He cracked a few eggs in a bowl and added in some milk. Satisfied with the texture, he poured the mixture into the heating pan. "I'm willing to bet you had some kind of out of body experience, crossing into some kind of alternate dimension. At least that's what I got out of the dreams I've been having lately. Kept seeing this guy who called himself Milord."

I almost jumped when he said that. "You saw him? What did he look like?"

David paused from stirring the eggs. "Let me see. He

wore dark green and had sort of reddish brown hair. His eyes were green too, if I remember right."

So Kishan had told me at least one truth. Milord was Christoph. I felt better having that confirmed. I still felt stupid for not connecting the dots sooner. But why hadn't he told me himself? I'm sure fooling me was not his original intention, now that I thought about it. After all, that first time I'd "met" Christoph in the little meadow, he had seemed rather surprised. And he'd known a lot more about me than he should have.

David wiped off his hands and took out another pan. "Sausage?" he asked and I shrugged. He pulled out a package of the little links anyway, lighting another burner to cook the spicy meat. "You know, come to think of it, if just anyone had told me that kind of thing, without my dreams, I might think they were crazy."

I tried to glare at him but it fell flat, even more me. "Thanks a lot."

David laughed. "Kidding." He stirred the eggs. "Not that I said you were crazy, just that anyone would think it." He turned off the burner with the eggs, blowing out the flame. "Mind getting some plates?"

I moved towards the cupboards. The extended relations always kept a supply of plates, cups, and silverware on hand. Our family never touched it though. Some of our relations were very picky. I didn't care as I pulled out two plates and brought them over to the stove. They could get mad at me all they wanted.

"So, what are you really doing here?" I asked as I put the plates down.

David served up the eggs, splitting them in equal parts. He added some sausages to each plate before turning off the other burner.

"Moral support," he shrugged and moved towards the table, a plate in either hand. "And to see for myself. Personally, I think the lot of them are the crazy ones. And just in case you wondered, I already knew you weren't

blood related. I've known since you were brought home."
He gave me an apologetic grin.

I accepted the plate he offered, and the apology, taking up the chair next to him. "Then you know I have to go back. Now that I know who I am."

He paused, fork stabbing into one of the links on his plate. "Yeah. I just wish I could go with you."

I stared at him. How could he want to come with me? He had no idea what I was about to face. Frankly, neither did I. The dream about Kishan standing in my way to the Waymeet was more than just a dream. Maybe it was a warning, or a premonition. I wasn't sure. But I knew I didn't want Kishan getting his fingers on my brother. I loved David too much to let that happen.

I guess he saw that in my eyes because he set his fork down and put one hand on my shoulder. "For as much as we have tormented each other all these years, I'm really going to miss you. And not just teasing you. I mean it, Kas. You've been more of a sister to me than any of the others. And I just want you to know that I'll always have your back, no matter what happens."

I wiped my eyes, trying to keep the tears from leaking out. "You big lug," I said and hugged him fiercely. "I'm going to miss you, too."

We talked about our childhood until around seven. I even helped him wash the dishes so he wouldn't get into trouble with the others. The autumn sun rose late these days and we both wanted as much time as possible to remember the good times we'd shared.

Just before eight, I almost reluctantly shouldered my bag. Thanks to David, I had a few more items packed inside, mementos from home and the like. He thought about everything. No wonder he was my favorite out of all my other siblings.

We didn't lock the door behind us. David promised he would later. I guess he wanted to straighten up some more. Maybe he just wanted to have some time alone.

Out of all my adopted siblings, he would be the one I missed the most. He had been my rock. I remembered all the times I'd run to him when I was young. It wasn't mom I wanted when I really needed comfort. It was David. Every girl needs an older brother. I was lucky enough to have him as mine.

We walked the path to the Sitting Rock in silence. The sun peeked over the trees as we reached the giant stone. The green jewel around my neck glowed. I pulled it out, stopping a few feet from the Rock. "He gave this to me," I explained as I took the chain off. "I want you to have it."

David looked up as I offered him the necklace. "You sure? I mean, if it was a gift from Milord."

I bit my lip. "Speaking of Milord, what did he say to you in those dreams you had?" I admit, part of me felt a bit jealous that he hadn't come to me. But then I realized it might have been Kishan's doing.

David took the necklace from me, letting the jewel dangle. "He told me about the Waymeet, and that you'd been there. He told me I should help you in any way possible because there was someone who would stop at nothing to harm you."

"Kishan," I whispered. I hoped he wouldn't show up again. But I knew he would. Maybe not today, but sometime down the road. It was part of my destiny.

My brother gave me a side hug as he ruffled my hair. "Don't worry, though. Big brother is here. Apparently there's something special about me that keeps him away."

I looked up at David with a bit of awe. Of course. Why hadn't I realized this before? David reminded me of Christoph. Christoph had reminded me of David. If they were of a similar vein, it made sense. They were both my protectors. One for this side of reality, one for the other. Except Christoph was so much more.

The sun climbed higher in the sky. But that didn't explain the sudden light I saw coming from just beyond the Sitting Rock. I turned towards that light and saw the a man walking towards us through the white rays.

"Who is that?" David almost stepped out in front of me but I held him back.

"Christoph," I breathed. I wanted to run into his arms but didn't trust my legs. He looked just like he had that first time I'd seen him in the meadow. My heart leapt inside my chest.

Christoph bowed, sweeping his cap in the all too familiar gesture. "Kas." He walked the remaining steps that separated us and took my hand, kissing it. He then turned to David. "Thank you for looking out for her all these years."

David gave a stiff bow back. He looked a bit wistful as Christoph continued to hold my hand. "It was my pleasure."

I broke free to hug my brother. "You dork," I whispered into his ear before breaking away. "Don't lose that stone," I warned. "I might want it back someday. And who knows? Maybe you can come and visit."

David laughed but promised. He moved to stand back as Christoph stepped forward once more.

"Are you ready?" Christoph asked. "From here on, life will be harder. You have a world to save, and a kingdom to reclaim. No matter what happens, I will remain by your side. And you will always have my love."

I swallowed, and then glanced at David for the last time, trying not to cry. I looked up into Christoph's eyes, which steadied me. "I'm ready."

Christoph nodded. He offered me his arm and I slid my hand around where his elbow bent. I saw my brother wave as we turned away from him. The light around us grew brighter as we walked towards it.

"I love you, sis," I heard David call out before we were completely engulfed in the light.

KEEP READING FOR A SPECIAL PREVIEW OF

Tarragon
Dragon Mage

KAS

KAS

ANWEN STARED OUT THE DIRTY window of the Volkswagen bus as it climbed the longest stretch yet. So far the scenery didn't leave much to the imagination. Especially not when she compared it to the descriptions from her great grandmother's diary. Yet again, she had to remind herself to slow down and remember they'd only just left the valley below.

She'd arrived in Blaucii on the Express only the day before. The city had been nice, full of the latest conveniences. And the hotel she'd stayed at had been more than welcoming.

The place she was going to now was pretty much guaranteed to have a less modern take on life. She wasn't excited about that. Already, she missed the warm beds and restaurants the city had to offer. Not to mention the transportation hub in the major parts of the city. She was sure they wouldn't have that in the village.

The low scrub hills blurred together as she thought about the previous stretch of her journey, the most enjoyable so far. The bullet train from Tawny Falls had held every modern convenience. It also had the most comfortable arrangements Anwen had ever experienced. She'd felt a little sad to bid the roomy Express goodbye. But she'd exchanged it for the less than ideal confines of the much older vehicle she now rode in. She tried to convince herself that it would all be worth it in the end.

Trying to find a more comfortable position on the depleted cushioning, she shifted her weight to one side. With a sigh, she gave up on the attempt and pulled out the diary, now much dog-eared and worn from constant reading. It was not hard to find the precise passage she wanted.

> *"I look forward to the time when we will see the Village of Lindwyrm once more, and the mountains of the Drakonii Range. Therein sits the ancient city of Tarragon, home of the Keepers. Though I have never seen it with my own eyes, I can picture it as if I had just been there. The mountains rise majestically all around. The sapphire blue waters of Lake Wyvern shimmer across the way, keeping sentinel over the Sacred Island.*
>
> *We Porters were once the Keepers of this place, living in a city of stone, the likes of which no one has seen in so many years. It is there that I hope, one day, to return, as we are destined to do. One day."*

Closing her eyes, Anwen shut the book. Her thumb traced the outline of the dragon pressed into the leather front of the book. The dragon's wings spread majestically above its turned head. Its tail wrapped around itself at the bottom, almost making a figure eight. She opened her eyes to mentally trace the pattern.

Noticing a subtle change in scenery, she looked out the window once more. Unable to place the exact difference, she pulled out the map she'd purchased down in the valley and set it in her lap. She tried to follow the thin line representing the road but wasn't sure where to start. She hadn't paid too much attention to their progress.

A pale, slender arm reached across the map and pointed at a bend in the line, causing Anwen to look up in surprise. It took her a moment to register that the young man who'd been sitting by her the whole time had finally moved. He'd sat as silent as a stone the entire ride. Asleep. Or so she'd thought. But his finger now pointed out their exact location on the marked paper, making her wonder.

"I believe we're about here," he said in a warm tone.

Anwen looked back down at the location he'd pointed to and nodded, trying not to appear as flustered as she felt. "I think you're right."

She looked up again to thank him, but paused as her hazel eyes met his brilliant blue ones. She noted his light brown hair and clear complexion. After realizing she was being rude, she shook her head, a faint blush forming across her cheeks. "Sorry. I didn't mean to stare."

He smiled. "It's all right. I get that reaction a lot, especially from people who don't know me." He held out his hand, gratified when she took it. "Allow me to introduce myself. I'm Tyler Durand. And you are?"

Trying not to blush even more, Anwen shook his smooth-skinned hand. Without thinking, she responded with her real name. "Anwen, Anwen Porter." Her fingers slid from his with a sort of reluctance, breaking contact. "Do you come this way often?" She winced at her own question.

Tyler laughed in amusement. "You might say something along those lines is true. What about yourself? Do you… come this way often?" His eyes sparkled in the sunlight as the bus crested one of the many lower lying hills of the Drakonii Range.

Anwen shook her head, her auburn hair falling to conceal her embarrassment. She looked up at, not his eyes, but his mouth. Looking into his eyes was dangerous. It made her stomach feel funny. "No, it's my first time. I guess you could say I'm trying to connect with my roots."

"Ah." Tyler nodded. "Yes, trees must establish firm roots if they are to grow. Visiting such roots only tends to strengthen them. Especially if one is willing to overcome the adversities of finding those roots, difficult as that task may be."

Anwen blinked in confusion and clutched at the diary. "Do you always talk in riddles?"

Tyler glanced out the window for a brief moment before looking into her eyes. "Only to those who intrigue me."

"Oh." Her heart beat like a jackhammer. It played a staccato so loud the driver could probably hear it, even though they sat all the way on the back row of the dilapidated bus.

Tyler shifted in his seat so he could look at her with greater ease. He crossed his arms over his chest as he surveyed the fair skinned girl in front of him. "You're definitely not from around this region," he explained. "I would know. But you have a familiar feeling of 'belonging' to you that I like. Few tourists have that."

Anwen decided to fold the map up and put it back in her bag, trying to ignore the attention she was getting from this complete stranger. "I'll bet you say that to all the girls who come visit."

He tilted his head back in thought, a far away look in his eyes. "To be honest, no. You're the first I've met in a long time who's felt like that..." He trailed off, looking troubled. Or maybe it was more thoughtful.

Anwen pursed her lips and slid the diary next to the map in her bag. "Well then, I guess that's not a bad thing, is it?"

Arms still crossed, Tyler leaned back against the seat. "No. But if I were you, I'd catch a nap while you still can. You might not get another chance before reaching the village. After all, tonight is a festival night." With that, he closed his eyes. His chest rose and fell with a hypnotic rhythm. The seat creaked a bit as the bus continued to climb the winding mountain road.

Anwen wasn't sure if he really was asleep or just faking, but decided to take his advice. She didn't know what kind of festival he meant, nor did she care. Even with the niceties of the bullet train, it had been hard to sleep. The simple truth was it wasn't her bed, not that the cushioned back seat was any better, but it would do. Holding her bag close, she closed her eyes and let herself drift with the passing clouds overhead.

ABOUT THE AUTHOR

Karlie Lucas is a graduate of Southern Utah University, were she received a Bachelor of Arts in Creative Writing. She is a member of Sigma Tau Delta, The International English Honor Society, ANWA, and SCBWI. She is interested in all things magical and mysterious, especially elves and dragons. She currently resides in the Dallas, Texas area with her husband.